BECAUSE OF YOU

Kay Ballard, a primary school teacher, obtained a position as companion to the children of Simon Nash, the composer ... But at Ashleigh, Kay discovered that the composer's home and background were surrounded by mystery. Three years earlier Simon Nash's wife had died in peculiar circumstances, out of which rumour had sprung and flourished ... How much of the rumour was false, and how much based on fact, became an obsession with Kay. And when the mystery was explained, danger and tragedy were in the air once more.

CATHERINE BRENT

◆

BECAUSE OF YOU

Complete and Unabridged

LINFORD
Leicester

First published in Great Britain in 1971 by
Robert Hale Limited
London

First Linford Edition
published 2006
by arrangement with
Robert Hale Limited
London

British Library CIP Data

Brent, Catherine
   Because of you.—Large print ed.—
Linford romance library
   1. Love stories
   2. Large type books
   I. Title
   823.9′14 [F]

ISBN 1–84617–262–4

Published by
F. A. Thorpe (Publishing)
Anstey, Leicestershire

Set by Words & Graphics Ltd.
Anstey, Leicestershire
Printed and bound in Great Britain by
T. J. International Ltd., Padstow, Cornwall

This book is printed on acid-free paper

1

Kay Ballard was settling down with no great enthusiasm to the breakfast of toast and poached eggs she had just prepared when she heard the plop of letters being thrust through the letter-box by the postman.

Placing her cup on its saucer and pushing an unruly tendril of raven black hair from her pale forehead, Kay went into the hall to collect the letters. There were two envelopes, she saw, one of them bearing Aunt Holly's immediately recognizable elegant script, the other a buff, official-looking envelope that had her address typed on it.

Settling down at the table once more, Kay decided she would force herself to eat before reading what Aunt Holly had to say. If she did not, and read the letter first, she knew she would be so upset afterwards as to forgo her meal, and she had skipped too many during the past fortnight for the good of her health.

Her mother had been dead for that length of time, and the void which Charlotte Ballard's passing had left in her life seemed something that would never be filled.

At the outset, when the woman was first stricken with the illness that was to prove incurable, Mrs Ballard had been lodged in the local hospital here in Westcroft, and Kay had been able to visit her most days when she had finished her work as a teacher in Moorfield primary school.

However, when her mother realized that the hospital and its staff had done everything that was in human power to do for her, she had requested to return home to her semi-detached villa on Woodstock Avenue.

'Don't you see, my dear,' she had said pleadingly to Kay, 'if I am not to get better, there is no reason why I should remain here in hospital. I would rather be at home, darling — in my own house. Anything that has to be done can be performed by our doctor and the local nurse. And I won't be a burden to you, I promise.'

The realization that her mother was aware of her condition proved a shock to Kay, and she had immediately been reduced to tears that she endeavoured, not too successfully, to conceal from the ailing woman.

She was not going to die, she argued with her mother. She was going to get well again, and much sooner than she anticipated. But if she really felt that she must come home, then Kay would try and arrange it.

Her mother had been brought home to Woodstock Avenue, and the doctor and nurse were in constant attendance. Still, as there were long periods throughout the early part of the day when the woman was completely alone, Kay was not at all happy about the arrangement.

Kay carried on with her work at the primary school. It was a strain of course. Always the hopeless condition of her mother weighed on her. Always she thought of those times when she was utterly alone in the house.

Her father had died five years before, and Kay was an only child. Their sole living relatives were Aunt Holly in Cornwall and her husband. Uncle Walter was anything but a robust man, constantly taking ill with a heart complaint, and so there was little that Aunt Holly could do for them even had she wanted to.

Mrs Collins, their next-door neighbour in the avenue, was a kindly woman, and looked in at Mrs Ballard at every opportunity. But Mrs Collins had her own husband and family of three children to care for, with the result that her perfectly good intentions were often frustrated.

At one stage Kay discussed with her mother the possibility of taking on a daily help. This Mrs Ballard would not hear of, much to her daughter's chagrin.

'Oh, no, my dear,' she had protested. 'For a start, we could not afford to hire a daily help. Your savings would soon be exhausted. Anyhow, I can manage quite well with things as they are.'

Kay had argued that they could afford to pay the wages of a help, for a little while at any rate. And even as she said this a coldness had taken possession of her heart. Her mother was adamant, so Kay dropped the subject.

Affairs reached their most crucial phase when, just a month ago, her mother had a turn for the worse. She must not be left alone, the doctor impressed on Kay. The local nurse would do what she could, but the only real solution the doctor could see was a return to hospital of the patient.

'But she won't go, doctor,' Kay had replied. 'She abhors the idea of having to leave home again ever, until — until — ' Kay could not finish her statement. She dissolved in tears.

'Then there is nothing else for it but that you look after her yourself, Miss

Ballard,' the physician had rejoined, sympathetically but firmly. 'You must give up your job for a while and remain in the house with her. I'm sure that if you explain there is no other alternative, your mother will agree to do what is sensible.'

Kay had not offered the sick woman the choice. Instead, without any delay, she had requested a leave of absence from her teaching duties on compassionate grounds. Her headmaster was kindly and understanding, and promised to take up her case with the education committee at once. The outcome was that Kay was granted an indefinite leave of absence.

'You can resume your duties when it pleases you to do so, Miss Ballard,' had been his concluding judgment. 'And I hope your mother recovers.'

Kay's mother had not recovered. Her illness had become worse, gradually at first, and then more rapidly. Prepared as she was for the inevitable, when it did come finally, the stunning shock was no less than it would have been had her mother died suddenly and without warning.

To help her achieve equanimity, Kay would have gone back to her work at Moorfield primary school at once, but the summer break-up and holidays were at hand. Before her she saw two long months stretching ahead of her, empty months during which she would sink deeper into despondency.

She did not have to sit at home and mope, of course. She could go on a long holiday — to the Continent perhaps. She had already been to Spain and Italy, and had enjoyed that holiday in Italy so much four years ago that she had promised herself to go back again.

But then, she had not been on her own during those marvellous vacations. She and Anne Bennet, who also taught at Moorfield primary school, had gone together. But Anne was married now and was taken up with a husband and baby.

At this stage Kay's thoughts had

swung to Barry Fielding.

Kay and Barry, who was a council housing official here in Westcroft, had met two years before at a dance. They had grown quite serious about each other after a time, Kay seldom going out without the young man as her escort, Barry continually ringing her up whenever he had a free afternoon. But then her mother had been taken ill and more and more of Kay's time had been devoted to the care of the woman, with the result that her blossoming friendship with Barry suffered seriously as a consequence.

At the outset the young man had been as she could have wished him to be — cheerful and patient. But as they saw less and less of each other their association weakened, and then one day went past without a telephone call from Barry, as did another and another.

Finally Kay was told by a well-meaning girl friend that Barry Fleming was seeing far more of a blonde by the name of Iris Milton than he was seeing of her, when Kay tried swallowing her disappointment and bitterness directed at fickle young men in general, and concentrated exclusively on her school duties and her mother.

On her mother's death Barry had called briefly to offer his condolences. He had made a feeble effort to take up the thread of their former relationship, but for Kay he had been tried and found wanting, and anything she had ever felt for him was gone beyond recall.

★　★　★

For the holiday period Kay could have gone to Cornwall and stayed with Aunt Holly and her husband. This idea soon lost its appeal however when she considered that Aunt Holly had enough to contend with without having her niece under her roof as a guest.

A few days later it had occurred to her that she could do much worse than get a job to fill in the vacant months before school commenced again. At this time of year students and lots of young people sought jobs in order to gain experience, while earning a little money to supplement their allowances. Of course she had no need for remuneration — not just then at any rate! — but she did have need of employment to lift her out of the trough she was presently wallowing in.

Once this idea had taken root, Kay asked herself what type of temporary work she would prefer doing. Store assistants were always in demand, as were people to help in the harvesting in country districts. Kay had finally studied the local newspapers and chosen three temporary situations more or less at random. She had then decided to wait for replies to her applications, and in the event of there being none — as was quite possible, she had been told — she would then call at some of the leading department stores in Westcroft.

A week had gone past since posting

her letters to the advertisers' box numbers of the newspapers concerned, and this buff envelope, she believed, contained a reply to one of her applications.

* * *

At length Kay gave up pretending she could wait until she had eaten before opening the envelope containing Aunt Holly's letter. Besides, no matter how hard she persuaded herself that she must eat her breakfast, she had little appetite for the meal. A change of routine and scene might work wonders for her appetite and her health in general. Would it be Cornwall for the months ahead of her after all?

'My dear Kay,' Aunt Holly had written, 'I trust that by this time you have recovered somewhat from the awful shock of your mother's death. Looking back to the days when we went to school together, I recall that it was I who was usually the weaker sister.

Indeed not a winter went past but I didn't suffer from the most terrible feverish colds. And here I am, as strong as the proverbial horse while your dear mother is gone! Kay, my sweetheart, I'm afraid I'm not striking the note I intended to strike. I intended that to be funny enough to bring a smile to your face, and I'm sure I've only succeeded in making you more miserable than you are. There I go again! The perfect light relief for any party!

'Seriously, darling, why not come down here and spend the summer with us? Uncle Walter is fairly well at the moment and joins me wholeheartedly in extending this invitation. What are you going to do about the house? Sell it? I wouldn't do anything too hasty if I were you, Kay. After all, it is a good house, and if you hang on to it you need never worry about having a roof over your head.

'There are so many things I wish to say to you, Kay, but I simply cannot think of everything at the moment. If you were to come down to Cornwall we could have a wonderful time, chatting and going around seeing things. Do please write soon and let me know how you are getting on, also if you can come and stay with us. Then we can make arrangements immediately.' The letter was signed, 'Your loving Aunt Holly.'

Kay read the letter through twice before folding it and sliding it into its envelope. She brushed a tear from her eye as she did so. Dear Aunt Holly. It really would be nice to spend the next two months with her.

At this stage Kay was tempted to revise her earlier decision regarding the trip to Cornwall. If Uncle Walter was in reasonably good health there was no need to feel guilty about being a burden to either of them.

All the same, she felt it wouldn't be the complete answer. She would rather get a job and immerse herself in work of some description. This would be the best method of regaining her perspective, she was sure.

Perhaps this meant she was being a trifle selfish, and thinking of no one but herself. But no, that wasn't true at all. She had never indulged her own whims or desires at the expense of anyone. And she really must get her feet planted firmly on solid ground again before the new school term commenced.

Now Kay laid her aunt's letter aside and poured a cup of coffee. Sipping it she unfolded the letter she had brought from the buff, official-looking envelope, her eyes widening when she realized the communication was from a firm of solicitors here in Westcroft, Baxter and Murdock, with an address on High Street.

'Dear Miss Ballard,' she read. 'We are replying to your application for temporary employment as children's companion, on behalf of the advertiser. In the event of your still being interested in the said employment, will you please call at our Westcroft offices on the 19th inst. between the hours of ten and twelve, a.m. or three and five, p.m. Should you have changed your mind or, for any other reason, are unable to attend an interview, it would be appreciated if you telephoned our offices at your earliest convenience.'

'The 19th inst.,' Kay murmured as her eyes scanned the letter once more. 'Why, today is the nineteenth of the month! Now where on earth did I put the clipping of this particular advertisement . . .'

She found it in the bottom of her handbag and sat down to peruse it as she finished her coffee. At the time of answering these advertisements she had been infinitely more confused than she was at the present moment. Well, perhaps confused was too strong a term to use. But she had been woolly-minded at least.

The wording of the advert in the situations vacant column ran, 'Intelligent young lady required to perform as children's companion for months of July and August. Cheerful seaside locality. Children aged ten and thirteen.

Would suit young teacher or student.'

'Ten and thirteen,' Kay mused as she took in the ages of the children for the first time. It was odd that children of these ages required anyone to act as companion during the school holidays. But perhaps the parents wished to go off somewhere by themselves and were anxious to leave their offspring in good and capable hands. 'Cheerful seaside locality? That sounds hopeful for a start. Besides, I enjoy the company of children far more than that of adults. Shall I give it a try? Why not, for heaven's sake! This could be the very medicine that the doctor ordered. But first of all I have to get through this interview with flying colours. Still, if I wasn't considered suitable I wouldn't have received this letter.'

Thus it was that, at ten-thirty that same morning, Kay, attired in a well-tailored costume that fitted her slim, but by no means skinny, figure to perfection, and wearing a trace of lipstick to brighten what she thought to be the wan pallor of her finely carved, heart-shaped face, presented herself to the middle-aged lady in charge of the reception desk at the offices of Baxter and Murdock, solicitors.

'Yes?' the lady murmured encouragingly, favourably impressed by the rather pale, large-eyed girl who approached her desk with a faint smile puckering the corners of her generous mouth. 'Is there something I can do for you?'

'I have an appointment for an interview,' Kay explained, feeling somewhat as she'd felt the first time she had gone for an interview to secure a job. She produced the letter she had received at breakfast and handed it over.

'Oh, yes. Miss Ballard . . . How do you do, Miss Ballard? Won't you take a seat while I see if Mr Murdock is free just now.'

Kay had been seated for only a moment when the lady emerged from an inner room and told her that Mr Murdock would receive her at once.

'If you'll come this way, please,' she invited.

Mr Murdock shot up from behind his desk as Kay was ushered into his presence and the door of the room was closed behind her.

'Ah, there you are, Miss Ballard!' the portly, balding man greeted effusively and extended his hand. 'I must apologize for the short notice you were given,' he went on with a wide smile, 'but it was due to an oversight. You should have been informed two days ago. Still, as you were able to make it . . . But do sit down, won't you. That's better! Now, where were we? Oh, yes! Mr Nash's advert for a children's companion. A temporary position, of course. You do understand that?'

'Yes, I do.'

'Good. Good! And I see by your letter of application which I have before me that you've been a teacher at a primary school here in town.'

'I *am* a teacher,' Kay amended. Suddenly she saw this whole thing as a rather foolish and unnecessary exercise. She didn't really require a job at all. Mr Murdock had gained the wrong impression from her application. What had she actually said in it in any case? He had assumed she was in dire need of a job, in dire need of the remuneration it would produce. Kay felt horribly hypocritical and her cheeks began to burn. At that moment she had an urge to jump up from her chair and rush out of this office, right out of the building. Also, she believed she was on the point of bursting into tears.

Somehow she must control herself. Somehow she must pull together her shattered nerves.

Mustering all her courage, she gritted her teeth firmly and smiled at Mr Murdock.

2

'Forgive me,' the portly solicitor beamed. 'Of course you are a teacher.' If he was aware of Kay's unease he gave no indication that he was. 'And I dare say you were thinking in terms of — shall we say, a working holiday?'

'That's right,' Kay returned shakily. 'Something of the sort. I do realize however that I would be expected to concentrate on whatever duties may be required of me, first and foremost. I am quite prepared for this.'

'I'm sure you are, Miss Ballard.'

Kay wondered if it wouldn't be best to unburden herself to the gentleman so that he might understand the better her reason for applying for a job in the first instance. Certainly Mr Murdock was old enough to have a family of his own — which he undoubtedly had — and would therefore be sympathetic towards her venture. Yet, on the other hand, might he not think a distraught person — or at least a person suffering from a mild depression, such as she unquestionably was — unsuited to the task of watching over two children whilst their parents were absent from home?

Naturally he would appreciate that her downcast mood was a temporary one, but would he go along with the idea that the course she had decided on was the correct one in the circumstances?

From somewhere — she knew not where — Kay conjured up a short laugh that actually sounded genuine and spontaneous to her own ears.

'I'm sure it strikes you as unusual for a teacher to jump from one job straight into another, Mr Murdock. Especially the sort of job that involves dealing with children.'

'Not really,' the solicitor smiled. 'I recall that, when I was your age, Miss Ballard, I was only perfectly happy when I was working. In any event,' he hastened on, making a steeple with his surprisingly long and slender fingers, 'your motivation is your personal and private business. Now, shall we get down to brass tacks, so to speak?'

This suited Kay immensely. 'By all means,' she agreed and waited for the interview to develop.

'Let me explain at the outset that Mr Nash decided to select you in preference to a dozen other applicants. We passed along all the applications that were forwarded by the Westcroft News and the Westcroft Examiner, naturally, and left it to him to make his choice. So at this juncture, may I congratulate you on your ability to put across something of your personality in writing, Miss Ballard.'

'Thank you!' Kay's cheeks were positively burning now. 'But Mr Nash hasn't seen me yet, and he may not — '

Here Mr Murdock gestured with his right hand in interruption.

'Not so, Miss Ballard. Mr Nash is an old friend of ours, and the fact is that he chose to leave the matter of the actual interview solely in my hands. Can I assume then that you are sufficiently interested to commit yourself? Remember that if you decide to back out at the last minute it will cause a great deal of inconvenience.'

'But I wouldn't dream of backing out at the last minute. I want this job, Mr Murdock. I must — ' Here Kay brought her lips together before she said something she might regret later.

'Good,' the solicitor acknowledged, evincing no desire to press her to enlarge. 'Mr Nash lives in Lynhaven — Oh, dear, I neglected to explain that the post is nowhere near Westcroft . . . But, yes, the advertisement did mention a seaside locality, if my memory serves me right. Then you were prepared to travel some considerable distance, Miss Ballard?'

'Yes, I was,' Kay answered. 'And as the nearest seaside town is fifty miles away, I had reckoned on a distance of that nature. Actually it is something in the region of sixty miles to Lynhaven, I believe.'

'That is so. It doesn't daunt you?' His eyes twinkled.

'Not in the least.'

Mr Murdock began to tell her about the train services she might use to take her to Lynhaven, but Kay informed him that she had her own car, and that if the job was hers she would go to Lynhaven by car.

'The job is almost certainly yours. However, before I can assume too much, I must tell you a little of the Nash family. Perhaps you have even heard of Mr Nash, Miss Ballard. I do know that only a few short years ago his name was on everyone's tongue.'

'Yes,' Kay returned thoughtfully. 'I'm sure the name ought to mean something for me. Of course! I've got it. Simon Nash . . . But no, it couldn't be that Mr. Nash.'

'But it is, Miss Ballard. Simon Nash, the composer of so many beautiful songs and melodies. As I say, and as you no doubt recall now, his name was a household word a few years ago. His songs are still well up in the — whatever you call it.'

'The charts?'

'That's right,' Mr. Murdock chuckled. 'The charts. Poor Simon! After it happened he seemed to lose his sparkle. His enthusiasm evaporated completely. They tell me that he can't even bear to glance at a piano these days. Most people imagine he left the country long ago. There was even a rumour last year that he had been killed in a car crash.'

'Yes,' Kay responded, roused out of her own dismal mood momentarily and feeling a quiver of excitement. 'I read about in the newspapers. There were, indeed, all sorts of rumours. Didn't — didn't his wife die suddenly?'

'Drowned,' Mr Murdock announced heavily and locked his slender fingers together. 'A tragedy. A terrible, terrible tragedy . . . '

Just then the whole thing came back to Kay. Yes, Simon Nash's wife had been drowned. She had gone out alone in a cabin cruiser and the boat had somehow caught fire. At the time the cruiser was some way from the shore, and the story went that Nash's beautiful wife had been overcome by fumes and eventually drowned.

There had been rumours surrounding the accident too. There had been an inquest at which some person purporting to be a witness had said he saw two people on the cabin cruiser a short time before it caught fire. This witness had steered his own boat to the scene, but arrived too late to do anything other than recover the woman's body from the sea. No trace had ever been found of this second person. No one else had been reported missing in the locality. The jury had declared an open verdict and the newspapers had made the most of the mystery. Then, eventually, as always happens, irrespective of the magnitude of the tragedy, it faded from the pages of the newspapers, and finally from the memories of their readers.

Kay's involuntary shudder told the solicitor that it was unnecessary to go over all the details.

'I believe you are familiar with the terrible accident, Miss Ballard?' he said tentatively.

'Yes, I am. Like almost everyone else, I had completely forgotten about it. It must have been an awful experience for Mr Nash, and no wonder he gave up composing afterwards. Still, I had no idea there was a family.'

'A boy and a girl,' Mr Murdock supplied. 'As was stated in the advertisement, the boy, Nicholas — or Nicky, as he is called, is ten years of age. His sister, Diane, is thirteen.'

'You know a lot about them, Mr Murdock.'

'Indeed I do. As I've told you, I know their father quite well, having always handled his legal affairs. You might wonder why he retains my firm as his legal advisers. The answer to that is a simple one. Mr Nash's father was an old friend of my late partner, Mr

Baxter. He is dead also, of course, but the younger Mr Nash decided to preserve the family link with our firm.

'The reason Simon needs only a temporary companion for the children is the fact that both of them are at boarding school in Bridgend. Naturally they both like to spend the summer holidays with their father. Occasionally they go abroad during those holidays. Last year they did. This year, however, they are remaining at Ashleigh, Mr Nash's home, you understand. Children of those ages rarely require an overseer, but the location of the house is such that there is the element of danger. Steep cliffs close to the house, coves where swimming is hazardous. I dare say that Diane could be trusted to keep within safe bounds, but not so young Nicky. Well, I don't have to tell you what boys of that age can get up to.'

'No, indeed,' Kay said with a faint smile. 'I know what they are.'

'I trust that what I have told you will

not put you off, Miss Ballard. And don't get the notion that Ashleigh is a perpetually dismal place. Far from it. Simon does have a circle of friends who drop in on him occasionally. His sister, Lorna lives in Lynhaven. She is a scientist at an experimental laboratory of some description. Simon's agent too has always kept alive their association. I believe it is his agent's burning ambition to encourage Simon to take up composing again . . . Well, there you are, Miss Ballard, I believe I've given you a thorough run-down on the background of your prospective employer. I might add that he keeps a cook who lives in, and a housemaid who lives out.'

Kay was deeply thoughtful when the solicitor had stopped speaking. She had not reckoned on involving herself in such a situation, of course. Despite the assurances of Mr Murdock, she had doubts regarding the wisdom of approaching such an atmosphere. Far from shaking her out of the misery which assailed her, living at Ashleigh, in the shadow of so much tragedy, might have the very reverse effect, even if there were two children to keep her occupied.

On the other hand, the job presented a challenge that she found vaguely attractive and stimulating. Perhaps a challenge of sorts was what she needed to enable her to forget the aftermath of her mother's passing. And she would be close to Simon Nash. She knew nothing about the man, practically, and had never laid eyes on him in her life. She had seen a newspaper photograph though, which presented him as a handsome, rather grave person, with austere mouth and expression of detachment. She knew his music thoroughly and had often compared it favourably with that of the late Ivor Novello. She even had a long-play record at home of such melodies as The Land of Roses and The Time of Beginning. She thought they were wonderful.

Mr Murdock clearing his throat

noisily brought Kay's attention back to the present moment.

'Well, Miss Ballard?' he smiled. 'I have the feeling that you would like a little time to think it over. Have a little time to do so by all means. But — '

'No, Mr Murdock,' Kay broke in impulsively. 'I will take the job if you think I shall suit Mr Nash.'

'You will? Splendid, my dear! I just know you will make the perfect companion for the two children. A combination of charm and firmness is what is required and I've seen enough of you to believe you have these qualities in full.'

'Thank you, Mr Murdock.'

'Thank *you*, my dear. Goodness! I'm relieved to get this load off my shoulders. If you hadn't said yes, I would have had to resort to taking the second person on the list. As a somewhat pernickety character, I detest having to settle for second best, no matter what the situation is.'

Kay could well accept this. At the

same time she wondered if the solicitor wasn't flattering her to some degree. She had the suspicion that what mattered most to Mr Murdock was that he send a reasonably capable girl to Ashleigh and so keep in Simon Nash's good books.

The portly solicitor smoothed his tie carefully and became briskly business-like.

'Now, Miss Ballard, regarding the salary that would be paid for your two months' work — '

'I'm sure it will be reasonable,' Kay broke in hastily. If her stay at Ashleigh served to shake her out of her present frame of mind, then she would be quite willing to commit herself for nothing more than her board and bed there. Once again she was tempted to divulge her story to the kindly gentleman, but once again she had reservations regarding the wisdom of doing so. 'What I mean is, that I don't expect the earth,' she resumed quickly. 'After all, I'm bound to derive some benefit from the change of scene.'

'Quite, quite! You are truly a remarkable young woman, Miss Ballard. Nevertheless, I am instructed on a certain course by my client, and I must acknowledge all my obligations. As I was about to say — the remuneration you can expect is a hundred pounds. It isn't a fortune by any stretch of imagination, but I do hope you will find it acceptable.'

'It is perfectly acceptable, Mr Murdock.'

'Good, good. Splendid! In that case could you take up your duties at the beginning of the month? The first of July, that is.'

Kay would have gone next day had it been necessary to do so. The sooner she set off, the less time she would have to ponder over her decision and entertain doubts. She nodded.

'Yes, I could,' she assured the solicitor.

He rose to his feet to indicate that the interview was at an end and Kay did likewise. After shaking hands once more he hurried round his desk to open the door for her. At that moment another thought appeared to occur to him.

'I almost forgot, Miss Ballard. Allow me to offer my deepest sympathy on the passing of your mother.'

Kay was completely taken aback.

'Then — then you knew?' she gasped.

'Yes, I did. And when such a misfortune strikes, usually the best thing we can do is get out and about and meet new people.'

'Goodbye, Mr Murdock,' Kay murmured from a suddenly constricted throat.

'Goodbye, Miss Ballard. I shall be in touch with Mr Nash without delay. Should you think of anything else that requires to be cleared up, please don't hesitate to get in touch with me. In the event of my not having a communication from you, I shall assume that all is going ahead as arranged.'

'You can take it for granted that

nothing short of disaster will stop me, Mr Murdock.'

'Good luck, my dear,' the solicitor said and saw her out.

★   ★   ★

The succeeding days seemed to drag heavily for Kay, and it appeared to her that the month of June would never run its course. She kept outdoors as much as possible, meeting a friend occasionally, and spending an hour chatting in some coffee shop or other. On the following Wednesday Anne Bennet, who was now Mrs Pringle, rang her up at lunchtime to invite her to spend the evening with her and her husband and baby.

'I feel rather guilty at neglecting you, Kay, darling,' Anne said. 'And Phillip and I were talking about you only last night.'

Kay laughed nervously into the receiver.

'I'm glad that somebody thinks of me, Anne. But no, I didn't really mean

35

that! These past few weeks have made me more introverted than ever. A trifle self-pitying too, I suspect.'

'Look who's talking about being an introvert! You were always one of the most outgoing girls I ever knew, Kay. Seriously, playmate, I hope you aren't spending all your time brooding about the past.'

'Nonsense!' Kay said quickly. Too quickly, she thought on reflection. 'But Mum's dying was a dreadful blow.'

'I know. Since giving up teaching to look after Phil and baby Carla, I've been out of touch with you and the rest of the gang. Which brings me back to tonight, Kay. How about getting together for a couple of hours and jawing over old times.'

'I'd love to, Anne. Thanks a million for asking me.'

'Oh, dear,' Anne Pringle worried, 'why didn't I ask you long ago! You sound shattered, my sweet.'

'Not really. What time would suit you?'

'Anytime after six would suit. Phil gets home from the office around six-fifteen. Listen, I'm cooking a big dinner this evening. Come early enough to share it. You still drive a car?'

'I couldn't do without it,' Kay laughed. 'Say six-thirty?'

'It's a date,' Anne chortled and hung up.

The evening with Anne and her husband turned out to be a real morale booster for Kay. Anne was avid for all the news pertaining to the school. Did Gloria still turn up in those shockingly short mini-skirts? Did old Mr Dickson continue to pick his teeth with a matchstick after his lunch? They laughed uproariously over their reminiscences. For the first time in days Kay's mood brightened.

'Talk about a stag night out!' Phillip Pringle observed at the end of the evening, when he helped Kay into her coat preparatory to her departure. 'It wouldn't hold a candle to this old boys' get-together. I've never seen Anne chuckle so much since she was plain Miss Bennet.'

'Oh, do come off it, Phil,' Anne remonstrated. 'You make me laugh too, but in a different sort of way.'

'Don't bother to tell me. Just let me guess. You get most of your amusement from watching me paddle from a warm bed to see why the baby is crying.'

Anne and Phillip really hit it off, Kay saw, and she couldn't help envying her friend just a little. To their request that she must make a return visit soon, she explained about the job she was taking for the holiday period.

'Companion to Simon Nash's children!' Anne ejaculated. 'Oh, golly, how I love that man's music. I would give anything to meet him in the flesh, darling.'

'Kay will tell you all about it when she gets back from Lynhaven,' Phillip grinned by way of consolation. 'But just watch how you go with Mr Music, Kay. They say he used to have all the ladies swooning in the aisles whenever he put in an appearance. He's a widower now, you know.'

'I do know, Phillip. But if you think for a moment that I'd let myself in for a grown-up family, you're crazy.'

'And, Kay, there's something else,' Phillip began seriously. He stopped speaking there and shrugged his broad shoulders. 'Never mind. You hear all sorts of queer stories about people, don't you? It's best not to bandy them around.'

His remark was cryptic enough to cause a worried frown to settle on Kay's brow as she drove away from the house. Was there more to the boating accident than she had heard? But even if there was, it was none of her business.

3

The first of July fell on a Tuesday. On Monday evening, as Kay was packing her cases to have them ready to stow in the car in the morning, the telephone commenced ringing. Wondering who could be calling her, she hurried to the instrument and announced herself.

'Kay Ballard speaking.'

'Oh, hello, Miss Ballard,' a deep voice greeted her. Even though she had never spoken to Simon Nash, she knew it was the composer at the other end of the line. 'Simon Nash here,' he said on the next instant, giving substance to her conviction.

'How do you do, Mr Nash?'

'How do *you* do, Miss Ballard?' A short laugh followed this, and then, before Kay could reply, 'I thought I should check if the arrangements you made with Mr Murdock, my solicitor, still hold good.'

'As far as I'm concerned, they do, Mr Nash. There hasn't been any change of plans on your part?'

'Good heavens, no!' Simon Nash laughed again. It was the sort of expression that came strange to him, Kay thought. It had a disturbing quality that sent an unaccountable tingle racing over her spine. 'Then I can expect you sometime tomorrow, Miss Ballard?'

'Yes,' Kay replied. 'I intend to leave just as early as I possibly can. Perhaps, indeed, I should have started out today so as to be there for tomorrow morning.'

'Nonsense. Your convenience suits me. And don't over-do it. The driving, I mean. Murdock told me you'd be travelling by car and under your own steam. Solo, that is.'

How did he imagine she would travel — with a companion to keep her out of scrapes? A boyfriend, perhaps?

'That is so. I rate myself as a reasonably competent driver,' she responded, wondering if he was using the exchange to weigh her up.

'I don't doubt that you are. All the same, please take your time so that you'll get here in a single piece. Part of the road you'll be travelling is in much poorer condition than it has a right to be.'

'Don't worry,' Kay told him. 'I'll be extremely careful.'

'Another thing, Miss Ballard,' Simon Nash went on. 'It's too much to expect you to easily hit on the direction to Ashleigh. We're right on the coast, you know. So if you get as far as the railway station, which you can't miss, I'll have someone there to meet you and lead you on to the house.'

'If you imagine it's necessary,' Kay said dubiously. 'But I'm sure I'll be able to find it without a lot of trouble.'

'I think it would be best all the same. But don't worry over keeping to any strict timetable. My lookout will not be impatient. If you just drive up to the front of the station and give a mild impression of being lost, he'll spot you without any difficulty.'

Kay joined in his amused chuckle.

'Very well, Mr Nash. Thank you for being so thoughtful.'

'Until tomorrow then, Miss Ballard. Goodbye for now.'

'Goodbye, Mr Nash,' Kay said and hung up.

Next morning turned out to be a gloriously clear one, with a pale blue sky that hinted of a fine day to come. Kay hoped the weather would prove a good augury for the two months that lay ahead of her. More than once she had pondered on Phillip Pringle's remark regarding the composer. What had Phillip started out to say that night, breaking off in mid-sentence and failing to conclude his statement? Kay had visited the Pringles twice since, but Phillip had evaded talking about the subject when she introduced it and left him the opening to resume commenting. Did he not wish to discourage her from going to work for Simon Nash, or was the answer simply that Phillip had heard the usual gossip circulating at the time of Caroline Nash's tragic accident, and reasoned it would be foolish to repeat it?

Now that she had spoken to the composer she felt less apprehensive about being in his employment at Ashleigh. The picture she had been forming of him was that of a cold, detached person who was so wrapped up in his own misfortune that he had forgotten there were other human beings in the world besides himself. The man she had spoken to sounded both kind and considerate, and she was certain that meeting him in the flesh would do little to detract from her revised concept.

She breakfasted lightly, settling for fruit juice, a soft-boiled egg and a slice of toast. She could well have set off without eating a scrap of breakfast, but common sense told her it would be silly to commence such a long drive without the fortification of some food in her stomach.

It was still barely eight o'clock and the air outside in the avenue, as yet unadulterated by car fumes and the horrible stuff that came from diesel-driven trucks, had the headiness of a finely flavoured wine.

Kay, unlike a lot of females that she knew, was fairly knowledgeable concerning the basic workings of a car, and checked the water and oil levels when her suitcases were stowed in the boot. With the two bulging suitcases in place the lid of the boot closed, but only just.

Afterwards she went about the house, taking care of all the little last-minute details she had endeavoured to file away in the back of her mind. Finally she made sure that every window was fastened and switched off the electricity at the mains. She had cancelled her milk delivery and informed her local police station of her proposed two months' absence. There had not been much need to do this, really, as Mrs Collins next door had promised to keep an eye on things. The woman had been delighted to learn of Kay's decision, agreeing that it was what she would do herself in similar circumstances.

At last all had been seen to and she had nothing more to do than step outside and close the door. She was on the point of doing this when the ringing of the telephone made her start.

Simon Nash again to say there had been some hitch to his plans? Surely not. The caller as it happened was Anne Pringle.

'I couldn't resist ringing you, Kay, to wish you lots of luck. I've just managed to feed Phil and the baby, and wondered if there was enough time left to call you. I suppose you will be getting under way shortly?'

'Oddly enough, you caught me in the act of closing the front door, Anne. I'm glad you did ring to say adieu. Thanks heaps for your good wishes. I'm fairly bursting with excitement, I can tell you.'

'I bet you are,' Anne laughed. 'But calm is the word, darling. You've had plenty of practise behind you. Calmness and patience was my motto when I was dealing with the kids at Moorfield. And watch the roads, Kay.'

'Will do. I'll tell you all about it when I get back home. It will give us something to natter about some evening.'

'That's something I'll look forward to. And, Kay, if you can collect a spare photograph for me I'll be delirious with joy.'

'You old fraud! Wait till Phillip hears of your secret passion. Give him my regards. And baby Carla of course. She's adorable. Anne.'

'Occasionally, I'll grant. Be seeing you, Kay.'

Kay had a warm flush in her cheeks as she went to her car and drove on to the road. Anne was such a sweet person, she thought. It was wonderful to have a husband and a baby. Well, it was what every girl hoped to have one day, wasn't it? Here Kay recalled Barry Fleming and knew a hurtful pang. Still, she had managed to get over Barry and she was glad that she had. Looking back now, she realized that it would have been the biggest mistake of her life had she eventually married Barry. Of course his memory had dimmed and she bore him no malice.

As she drove past the front of her neighbour's house, Mrs Collins waved from a window and Kay waved back. She wasn't really alone in the world after all, not when she had such good friends as Mrs Collins and the Pringles.

Kay made her first halt at a service station, where she had the petrol tank filled and asked the attendant to check the pressures of her tyres.

'Shall I look at the oil when I'm at it?'

'The oil level is all right, thank you.'

Ten minutes later she was leaving Westcroft behind her, and soon reached the main road going south and east that would finally take her to Lyndale and the home of Simon Nash.

★ ★ ★

Kay made one stop at the village of Paxton, an enchanting little backwater roughly half-way to her destination. Here she had a cup of coffee and a sandwich at a charming coffee shop in the centre of the village. Refreshed, she strolled about for a few minutes to stretch her limbs.

The advancing morning was fulfilling its earlier promise and the sun shone warmly on neat flower gardens and the three great chestnut trees which were a unique feature of the village.

Renewed both physically and mentally, Kay went back to her car and began the second stage of her journey. This second half appeared to be much longer, but when she glanced at her wristwatch on the approach to the outskirts of Lynhaven she saw that she had actually taken less time on covering the latter section.

As Simon Nash had indicated, it was easy to find the location of the railway station. Almost everywhere were signs pointing towards it, and when Kay drove on to the wide parking area before the station buildings she realized why. Hundreds of people were coming off trains; the trains themselves seemed to be shuttling in and out with great regularity. Taxi cabs were doing a roaring business, and Kay had scarcely halted when three touring coaches swept up in the sunshine, washed and polished and with the paintwork gleaming. It appeared to be a signal for a huge party of Girl Guides to emerge from the station environs under the watchful eye of their leader. Certainly Lynhaven was a popular holiday resort, and just then was reaching the peak of its season.

Kay was considering nipping into the station to buy a newspaper or magazine, for little other reason than to give herself the opportunity of looking around. Ever since she had been a small girl on her first outing with her father, railway stations and trains exerted a fascination on her, and she could seldom resist seeing what a strange station looked like. There was rarely much difference to be seen between one railway terminus and another, but each had its own peculiar hustle and bustle and all had an oddly charged atmosphere that Kay found attractive and stimulating. She had alighted from her car when a voice spoke behind her.

'Excuse me, Miss. Would you be Miss Ballard from Westcroft?'

Kay wheeled suddenly to look at the elderly, ruddy-cheeked man who confronted her. There was an air of the outdoors about him and Kay immediately slotted him into the category of gardener. His next words spoken with a wide smile proved her judgment to be correct.

'I'm George Mallows,' he introduced himself. 'Part-time gardener at Mr Nash's place.'

'How do you do, Mr Mallows. Yes, I am Miss Ballard, and I dare say you have come here to act as my guide to Ashleigh. I'm sure I could have found my way, but it was considerate of Mr Nash to make it easy for me. You've got a busy town here, Mr Mallows. Holidaymakers are coming in from every conceivable direction.'

'That just about sums it up,' the other grinned. 'We'll have this now right through till the end of September. After that things settle back to normal again.'

'Normal?' Kay laughed. 'I would have thought you'd call this present situation normal. But I do see what you mean. Well, shall we proceed to my destination, Mr Mallows. You do have a car?'

'Over there,' the man agreed and gestured to a gleaming black Rover. 'It's Mr Nash's car,' he chuckled when he saw the look of surprise which crossed Kay's features. 'Something smaller serves my purpose. Shall we be off then? You won't have much bother keeping up with me, as I don't drive that fast.'

All the same, as the gardener set off in the Rover and Kay moved into his wake, she saw that he drove fast enough, and with a skill that would have made a much younger person envious.

Their course took them through the centre of Lynhaven and along the main street that dipped right to the sea. The sea was marvellous, Kay thought, a deep blue beneath the glorious sunshine. There were yachts scudding before the breeze, rowboats by the dozen in closer to the shoreline. There was a wide promenade that stretched apparently to infinity on either side, where people either strolled or took their ease on the dozens of benches scattered about. All in all it was a perfect holiday resort, Kay felt.

Now Mr Mallows was turning off the road flanking the promenade, taking a right-hand bend that led them through a quieter area of the town. Here staid bungalows and villas lined the streets and avenues. Now they were in a shopping centre again, and Kay began to understand why Simon Nash had deemed it wise to provide her with an escort to his home.

Five minutes later the town lay behind them. Out there on Kay's left the sea billowed and rolled to the horizon. On her right were hedgerows hemming in fields and colonies of summer cottages and caravans. Gulls dipped and swooped, and with the windows partly open as they were, their shrill cries penetrated to her ears. And what with all this and the salty tang in her nostrils, Kay had a sensation of uplift, of renewal, of a falling away of the despondent mood which had held her a prisoner for so long now. She was on the verge of a new scene, with new people whose lives would be part of her own — for a little while at any rate — and she believed she would benefit vastly as a result.

Ashleigh was a large house brooding in what Kay judged to be three or four acres of ground. A driveway led from the entrance gates and wound through lawns, shrubbery and flower-beds to a tarmac forecourt. The house was not a new one by any means. It would have been standing here for fifteen or twenty years, at least, Kay guessed. The walls were grey and would have presented a more pleasant aspect had they been cleaned down and transformed to a brighter hue. Three stone steps led up to the front door, and the two cars had no sooner come to a standstill than an inner door opened and a tall, rather distinguished looking man who would be about thirty-five or so, Kay imagined, emerged. With him were two children, a boy and a girl, who took a few steps before halting and staring whilst their father — who else could they be but Simon Nash and his son and daughter? — came to greet her.

'Well, here we are, Mr Nash,' George Mallows boomed in his cheerful voice.

'I found Miss Ballard at the railway station as soon as I arrived.'

'Thank you, George. How are you, Miss Ballard? Not too tired after your long journey, I hope?'

'Not really,' Kay said. Simon Nash had little flecks of grey at his temples, she saw. But he was a youthful, virile figure for all that, with an odd magnetism in the dark eyes that seemed to encompass her for a brief instant, assessing her against what he already knew of her, no doubt. Apparently he was satisfied with what he saw. A smile blossomed on his clean-cut somewhat stern features and he extended his hand.

'What did you think of Lynhaven? You've never been to this part of the country before?'

'No, I haven't. Lynhaven strikes me as a wonderful town. So bright and — and gay just now.'

'Yes,' Simon Nash chuckled. 'Gay is the word. It's a positive mecca for holidaymakers, you know. They come here every summer in their tens of thousands and take over during their stay.'

Did she detect a trace of resentment when he referred to the holidaymakers? But possibly there were others who were equally resentful of the annual invasion.

Kay permitted her gaze to sweep past the composer to the two waiting children.

'And this young lady and young gentleman will be Diane and Nicholas, I gather?'

'Your problem for the next couple of months, Miss Ballard,' the other laughed. 'Come here, you two, and say hello to Miss Ballard.'

The girl was slim and fair, with a wealth of silken hair to her shoulders and the bluest eyes Kay had ever looked into. As those blue eyes met her own Kay had the sensation of being appraised shrewdly. The mobile face remained still for a moment before wreathing into the most enchanting smile, showing small white teeth.

'How do you do, Miss Ballard?'

'Hello, Diane,' Kay said warmly, glad that the girl had accepted her. 'Hello, Nicholas,' she added as she turned to look at the boy.

'How do you do, Miss Ballard,' Nicholas responded shyly. Like his father, the boy was dark and possessed of that somewhat severe clean-cut profile. Both children were clad in slacks and sweater and it was obvious they had been preened up for this encounter.

'All right, kids,' Simon Nash said gruffly, 'off you go and carry on cycling. But remember what I told you about staying clear of the cliffs.'

'Don't worry, Dad,' Diane replied with another searching sidelong glance at Kay. 'I'll see that Nicky doesn't go near the cliffs. I'm so glad that you're here, Miss Ballard,' the girl added impulsively while colour stained her cheeks.

'Me too,' Nicholas declared, his shyness forgotten. 'And you aren't old at all.'

Kay found herself blushing as the pair of them tore off round the side of the house where the garage stood. A low laugh from Simon Nash caused her to bring her gaze back to him.

'Just a joke, Miss Ballard. Nancy has been brainwashing him to some extent. Nancy is the maid. She told Nicky that the lady who was coming to keep an eye on him would be old and ugly, and would rule him with a rod of iron.'

'I see! Well, I'm glad that Nicholas is relieved. At least I hope he doesn't find me too old and too ugly, and I really haven't brought a rod of iron along.'

'I think you'll fill my bill to a T, Miss Ballard,' Simon Nash smiled. 'And now, I'll help you in with your baggage, if I may. Then I'll have Nancy show you to your room. You're bound to want to freshen up and rest a while. Also, you're ready for your lunch, I'll warrant.'

A little later Kay was being led into the big house, Simon Nash carrying her suitcases as though they weighed nothing at all.

4

The long entrance hall appeared to run half the width of the building. Off it doors opened on a drawing-room, a library, a living-room, in that order.

'I'll leave your cases here and show you the ground floor. This was my father's house before it became mine, Miss Ballard, and I'm afraid that little has changed since he and mother held sway. I've been tempted once or twice to sell it and move into a more modern residence. However, I've always changed my mind, and on the last occasion I did so I had central heating installed as a sort of compromise.'

'It shows that one half of you, at least, would rebel against moving. Personally, I rather like the location. You are close to the sea and the country, and there's lots of privacy if you're inclined to seclusion.'

'It has its advantages.'

Kay wasn't sure whether he was talking about the house or the seclusion. He continued to speak.

'My parents used to be country dwellers, you know. Father was what you might have called a gentleman farmer. Mother was a singer in those days — before she met my father, naturally. Music hall stuff, you understand. She wouldn't have made much of a name for herself at the present time,' he finished wistfully.

'Then — then your parents are both dead?'

'Years,' Simon Nash murmured. 'I believe you lost your mother recently, Miss Ballard.'

So Mr Murdock had passed on all he had gleaned about her background!

'Yes,' she said. 'That's so. It's partly the reason for my wanting a change of scenery.'

'I understand. That's life, isn't it. I was telling you about my mother. She went by the name of Nell Howard.

Howard was her maiden name.'

'Nell Howard?' Kay repeated, trying to recall if she had ever heard of the singer. 'I must admit it doesn't ring any bells. You, however, are something different.'

He gave her a sharp glance before smiling wryly.

'So you have heard of me? Yes, you likely have . . . Well, let's start with the drawing-room, shall we? By the way, you're probably more ready for a break to refresh yourself than — '

'Of course I'm not tired,' Kay protested, as indeed she was not. Arriving at this house and meeting this man had the effect of banishing any weariness she might have felt as the result of her long journey. Most of her preconceptions had been proved wrong.

The furniture, Kay discovered, toned in with the general mood of the house, being aged and solid, and constructed for convenience and comfort rather than for any aesthetic purpose.

When they reached the library Simon

Nash produced a bottle of sherry and glasses from a cabinet, and offered Kay a cigarette as well. She acepted these and gazed at the masses of books on the shelves which occupied three walls of the room.

'You have an interest in books, Miss Ballard?' he murmured.

Some inflection in his tone caused Kay to pause with her glass at her lips to catch him studying her intently. Suddenly she felt that tingle along her spine that had manifested itself when she'd spoken over the telephone with the composer last night.

'Nothing inordinate,' she replied. 'My reading taste could be described as Philistine. The occasional detective novel, the odd travel book or biography. Of course I have the usual brush with the classics. Nothing really to boast about.'

'Being a schoolteacher, you would naturally have to cover a wide range. Do you enjoy being a schoolteacher, Miss Ballard?'

The directness of the query had the effect of putting Kay off balance momentarily. But directness of approach would be one of this man's characteristics, she decided, welcomed or not.

'Yes, I do,' she answered. 'I'm fond of teaching and I enjoy the company of children. Working at a primary school provides me with enormous satisfaction.'

'And you would never dream of changing your job?'

Strangely, it was the first time that anyone had ever suggested such a thing; the first time too that Kay had ever paused to consider whether she would like a change. Her negative headshake was almost instinctive.

'Goodness, no!'

'You say that aggressively,' Simon Nash smiled. 'As though you resent even the bare mention of the idea. It's queer, you know, how people allow themselves to slide into ruts and they pretend to themselves and the world around them that they could never make a change under any circumstances.'

'Are you certain you've got your facts right?' Kay queried with a trace of sharpness in her voice. And wasn't he resisting change?

There was the faintest hint of mockery in the composer's eye. 'I believe that I have. Let me enlarge, Miss Ballard. People don't cling to these ruts that I've spoken of simply for the love of them, not even for the sense of security they may derive from endless repetition. Oh, no! The problem is deeper rooted.'

'Indeed! Why do they cling to their ruts then, Mr Nash?'

'Fear,' Simon Nash said on a note of triumph, and paused to allow Kay to challenge his statement if she dared. The bait was much too tantalizing for Kay to resist.

'Oh, come now, Mr Nash. Surely not! Fear of whom? Fear of what? I confess I see few people cringing in their little gloomy ruts. Are you supposing that they present a bold face to the world while inwardly trembling because of goodness knows what?'

'Fear of change,' Simon Nash expanded. 'Fear of the new and the unknown. If only people were more bold, more willing to accept innovation, more willing to experiment.'

Such nonsense, Kay thought. Had he forgotten about all the feats that mankind had so far achieved? Had he never heard of the men who had gone to the moon? Or were his remarks intended for a restricted context, and aimed at young women like herself?

'You are saying therefore in effect, change my job and I shall attain new heights in experience? Not seriously, Mr Nash?'

'Of course not! Not unless you feel the compulsion for a change. But when you do, I think you should yield to it.'

'There we differ, I'm afraid,' Kay declared, determined to stick to her guns. 'In such a case as you mention, my advice would be to examine every angle carefully before making any definite move — '

'Caution again, Miss Ballard'.

'Why not, Mr Nash? Surely there is as much merit in being cautious as there is in being impetuous? And what about yourself?'

'Now you are blurring the issue. How like a woman to impute what was never intended!'

Kay was at the point of retorting when she realized that she had only met this man, and that, moreover, for the next two months he would be her employer. Therefore, if they started off their relationship with a sparkling clash of wits, it might colour everything to her disadvantage. If Simon Nash was eager for an intellectual skirmish he would have to seek elsewhere for an opponent. She was here in the capacity of companion for his children, and was reluctant to attempt filling any other role that might cause embarrassment at a later date.

The composer's hearty laugh rendered her reservations to the level of the ridiculous. Had he merely been making fun after all?

'I'm sorry, Miss Ballard. Forgive me. Once I get going on a pet subject I'm liable to reduce you to a tantrum or tears. And since you've only arrived, I must spare you the discomfiture of either. A little more sherry?'

'Thank you, no.'

Even as Simon Nash appeared to sober, it was difficult to tell whether he wasn't secretly laughing at her. When she put her cigarette to her lips he held a lighter for her. She would have sworn an imp of mischief was dancing somewhere behind those dark eyes. Doubts assailed her briefly.

They both turned to face the door when a loud voice sang along the hallway, startling Kay somewhat.

'Hello, the house! Isn't anyone at home?'

'That will be Bruce,' Simon Nash frowned. 'Bruce Manson, my cousin.

I'm certain the blighter has dropped by with no other motive in mind than seeing if my companion has turned up.'

'*Your* companion, Mr Nash?'

'Dash it, Miss Ballard, you understand what I mean. And here if I may offer a word of warning, beware of my cousin, Bruce. He is under the delusion that beautiful women are meant to be eaten.'

'I heard that last remark, you know,' Bruce Manson said briskly from the doorway. 'It's less than fair, Simon.'

'Perhaps. But I dare say Miss Ballard is equipped with the necessary ability to judge for herself. Since there doesn't appear to be a suitable alternative, Miss Ballard, meet my cousin. As I've told you, his name is Bruce Manson. Miss Ballard, Bruce.'

'How do you do, Miss Ballard? It is Miss Kay Ballard, I've been given to understand?' Manson smiled.

'That is so, Mr Manson.'

'Bruce, Miss Ballard, please.'

'Very well,' Kay said and joined in his

chuckle. When she made no move to hold out her hand Bruce Manson extended his own, holding on to her fingers for slightly longer than was absolutely necessary. His admiration was obvious.

He was a very tall man, an inch at least over six feet, Kay was sure. He was fair and blue-eyed, with thick brows that had a habit of arching quizzically when he was amused. For an instant Kay wondered whom he reminded her of, and then thought of Diane.

He tossed a glance at Simon Nash and began to explain. 'I just happened to be driving past your front gate, Simon, when I came over devilish thirsty and wondered if you'd have anything to allay a parched condition.'

'Help yourself,' Simon Nash invited. 'There's little but a spot of sherry in the cellar at the moment. But I'm sure it will do to be getting along with.'

'Thank you, Simon. Can I freshen up your glass, Miss Ballard?'

'No, thanks,' Kay said. 'Mr Nash was

showing me over the ground floor of his house — '

'He ought to put a match to it. I mean it,' the young man went on when Kay simply stared. 'Wouldn't you be tempted to do likewise if you owned the old barrack, Miss Ballard?'

Kay's cheeks heated. Joking or not, it was patent by the frown of annoyance that Simon Nash displayed that this was a tender spot with him. She hastened to answer his grinning cousin.

'No, I wouldn't. I think it is rather a fine building. The location is simply wonderful — '

'The location, perhaps,' Manson broke in. 'But not the building which occupies it, surely? I've been on at Simon to make a clean sweep and erect something more in keeping with the times in its place. I know that I would, were I in his shoes.'

'There is the kernel of the matter, my dear Bruce. You are not in my shoes. Heaven forbid that you should be. Well, Miss Ballard, shall we continue? You're bound to be both tired and hungry. I want to introduce you to Nancy and Mrs Foley. I believe they're in the process of preparing lunch.'

'Did I hear you say lunch, Simon?' Bruce Manson queried over the rim of his glass. 'I haven't had a bite since dawn, apart from the traditional bowl of cornflakes and coffee.'

'You're welcome to join us, Bruce, if you've got the time to spare.'

'Oh, I've got all the time there is,' Manson rejoined blithely. 'Did a first-class job for our last client, and the boss is ready to offer me any concession I care to mention.'

'That must be very nice for you,' Simon commented drily.

'I'm in advertising, Miss Ballard,' Manson gushed on as his cousin propelled Kay to the door of the room. 'Write copy and stuff like that.'

'It must be a very interesting occupation, Mr Manson.'

'Oh, it is! I'd like to tell you all about it sometime.'

'Some other time, Bruce,' Simon Nash insisted. 'Please excuse us.'

'Of course. You're a schoolteacher yourself, I've heard, Miss Ballard?' Manson was intent on dragging this out.

'I work at a primary school in Westcroft,' Kay replied.

'That should be interesting too, I'm sure. But more amusing than interesting, I bet?'

'It has its moments. Goodbye, Mr Manson.'

'Until lunch,' the other reminded her. 'Thanks for having me, Simon, old chap.'

'Make yourself at home,' Nash invited icily.

Kay had little time to analyze their relationship just then, for Simon Nash guided her from the library and on to the kitchen at the rear of the house. The odours which exuded reminded Kay that she really was hungry. Her companion gave the door a tap before opening it. A jolly-looking woman was working at steaming pans whilst a younger woman in a housemaid's uniform was taking crockery down from shelves.

'Mr Nash,' the older woman began scoldingly without turning her head, 'you know how I hate intrusions when I'm busy in my kitchen.'

'Yes, I do, Mrs Foley. But I imagined you'd be able to spare a second to say hello to Miss Ballard.'

'Oh, my dear, I'm sorry!' the woman apologized to Kay. 'But things haven't been going too well for me today, Mr Nash. It's this cooker.'

'The cooker? Well now, what has happened to the cooker? To my eyes it's operating remarkably well at the moment.'

'That's just the whole point. It's operating far too well. I'm sure there's something wrong with the thermostat. No matter how low I set it, it will keep burning things.'

'Then we'd better have an electrician give it the once-over, Mrs Foley. I'll endeavour to make arrangements as soon as possible.'

'I wish you would.'

The cooker was an extremely old model, Kay saw, and wondered at Simon Nash not installing a more modern one. Was he so hard up that he couldn't afford the expense of a new cooker? If so, then it might explain a lot — the old house, its need for exterior renovation. On the other hand, the composer could be a tight-fisted person, reluctant to spend more money than he actually had to. Or an eccentric? another thought intruded. Well, she had his performance in the library to base this premise upon. Bruce Manson might prove enlightening on the subject.

Nancy, the maid, was a trim brunette of about twenty-five or so, and greeted Kay cheerfully. She said she would show Kay to her room upstairs immediately she had laid the dining-room table, if she could wait that long.

'There is no hurry,' Kay assured her.

'Look,' Simon Nash suggested, 'I'll carry your cases up at any rate, Miss Ballard. 'I can indicate your quarters while I am at it.'

This he did, showing Kay the room she would occupy in the west wing of the house. Originally it had been intended as a guest room, the composer told her, and was complete with its own adjoining bathroom.

'I do hope you will be comfortable, Miss Ballard. Should there be anything not to your liking, I trust you will let me know.'

'Thank you, Mr Nash. I have the feeling that I'm going to like everything here. Your children are adorable. I can't wait to get to know them properly.'

'Don't worry. You soon shall. I'd say they're busily discussing you at this moment. But as you're not so old as Nicky was led to expect, and as you don't control with a rod of iron, I'm certain their conclusions will all be in your favour.'

Simon Nash left her and Kay took

stock of her quarters. The room she was to occupy was a trifle larger than her own bedroom back home at Westcroft. There was a comfortable looking bed, an old oak dressing table with an oval mirror, a built-in wardrobe which was surely an innovation, and the wide window offered a view of green lawn stretching to a wooden fence, beyond which, by standing on her tiptoes, Kay could see the white breakers racing in to the cliffs. The vista was delightful.

'Nice and cosy,' she murmured to her reflection in the mirror when she had washed and changed into a new blue dress and was brushing out her hair. 'And if I had something solid to eat I imagine I'd be quite ready to face anything that Ashleigh cares to present.'

At lunch in the dining-room she and Simon Nash were joined by the two children and Bruce Manson. The children addressed Manson as Uncle Bruce and indeed seemed to treat him as though he were their uncle.

All through the meal he regaled them

with stories relative to his job at the advertising agency. He was something of an artist as well as a copy-writer and produced lightning sketches of some of the agency's clients, using a ballpen and scraps of notepaper.

'This is Mr Q. A very pompous person. I daren't divulge his real name for fear of being sued. He strides into my office one day and says he's got a super-duper idea for promoting his string of hair-dressing salons. There was this bunch of hippies, you see — our long-haired and flower-decorated brethren, for the benefit of the unitiated — and they decide to rebel against the rebellion that had already transformed them into hippies. So one of them says to the other, 'We'll get our hair cut and make ourselves really beautiful, Charlie — ''

'Was his name really Charlie, Uncle Bruce?' Nicholas wanted to know.

'Of course it wasn't, Nicky. You don't want me to be sued, do you? Anyhow Charlie asks his friend which hair-dresser they should go to, and can you guess what his friend replies?'

'Mr Q?'

'Correct first time, young man.'

'Did you use the idea?' Diane asked next.

'Of course I didn't, darling. I explained to Mr Q that his was the best recipe for going bankrupt I'd heard in years.'

The children laughed, as did Kay, but more from a desire not to hurt Bruce Manson's feelings than from any amusement she felt. There were other such anecdotes throughout the meal, stories which Simon Nash seemed to bear with a detached tolerance.

5

Bruce Manson didn't stay long after lunch was over. Despite the supposedly good terms shared by him and his boss, he declared that he must at least put in an appearance at the offices of the advertising agency.

'Well, you don't like to take advantage, do you?' he said to his cousin and Kay. 'After all, I am dependent on my job, to a certain extent.'

'He can say that again,' Simon Nash mused when Manson had gone to his car. 'If he lost the position he has at Fleece's, he'd have bother finding one as good.'

'But if he's an expert copy-writer, shouldn't he have a wide open field to choose from?' Kay was urged to comment. She thought Bruce Manson quite handsome and a pleasant enough companion. His antics with the children had been in the nature of a display to attract her attention, she believed. He wished to impress on her as well as on them that he was a thoroughly decent chap and relatively innocent and guileless, and even if his efforts had been transparently obvious, it could scarcely be said he had committed a sin.

Actually he had created an impression on Kay. She enjoyed the company of men who could laugh easily and who tried to be amusing themselves. With the going of Bruce from the house it was as though he had taken a harmless gleam of sunshine with him.

'Oh, he is a passable copy writer,' the composer agreed. 'But unfortunately he isn't exactly the genius he would have people think that he is, nor is he as industrious as he pretends to be at times.'

Did Kay detect a trace of envy in Simon Nash just then? But why on earth should the composer be envious of his cousin? Because of his easy manner and his infectious good nature? Because of the way he appeared to treat things lightly — Eat, drink and be merry, for tomorrow is a new day? Or was there some other reason that she couldn't guess at, not being conversant with the overall context as yet?

She realized it would be unwise to pursue the subject, and in any case, Bruce Manson's business was his own, as far as she was concerned.

'The children certainly get along with him,' she said.

'Yes, they like their Uncle Bruce. I suppose it bears out the theory that a teller of tall tales will always be assured of ready ears to listen to them.'

This remark Kay thought to be somewhat unfair also, but as she had made up her mind to remain neutral for the present, she resisted any temptation she might have had to argue.

Later that day she had the opportunity of getting to know Mrs Foley and Nancy better. They had a friendly chat over cups of tea, when the conversation covered things generally pertaining to Ashleigh.

'It's bound to be a little strange to you at the beginning,' the homely cook said with a smile. 'But you'll soon adjust.'

'Isn't everything strange at the beginning?' Nancy laughed. 'When I first came to the house to work, I had the feeling that a month might do me.'

'Perhaps it was being away from the centre of town made you feel so,' Kay hazarded. 'You've settled in now, of course.'

'And how! Mr Nash is the most considerate employer a girl could hope to have. Naturally the place is busier in the summer, when the two kids are at home. But it's also a lot brighter as well. Isn't it, Mrs Foley?'

'I confess I cry my eyes out when the time comes for them to go back to their boarding schools. They'll give you precious little trouble, Miss Ballard, I'll warrant.'

Kay had already decided on this and

she said so. If she expected that either Mrs Foley or Nancy would make reference to the late Mrs Nash, she was mistaken, and assumed that Simon Nash's wife and the boating accident which had caused her death were taboo. Or perhaps they had simply forgotten it.

Once again she reflected on the story as had been made known to the interested world via the newspapers, and the rumours which had blossomed afterwards. But, she told herself, whenever a tragedy of this nature occurred, rumours seemed a natural attendant to the aftermath. For her own part, she had no time for rumours or any other sort of ill-founded gossip.

Kay hardly saw the children at all that first day at Ashleigh, and came to the conclusion that Simon Nash wished her to have enough free time to make an appraisal of her surroundings and settle in properly before being burdened with responsibility.

She turned in early and slept soundly enough until, at around two o'clock in the morning, she came awake with the sensation that some noise or other had disturbed her. Sitting up in bed, she switched on the bedside lamp and shivered momentarily in the eerie stillness. Surely her imagination wasn't playing tricks on her? Had she been dreaming of something unpleasant, and had unconsciously willed herself to came awake?

A board squeaked beyond the door of her bedroom and she stiffened. There was the noise that had disturbed her! Somebody was on the prowl in the house. Even as she held her breath the better to listen, she heard the creak of a door prior to the sound of its gentle closing.

For a wild moment Kay wanted to scream. She soon had her panic in check however. She was far from being an hysterical person, and it would take infinitely more than a squeaking floorboard and a creaking door to frighten her. It only meant that Simon Nash was making his rounds before turning in for the night.

At two o'clock in the morning? Surely not!

All the same, it was none of her business. There were other people in the big old house besides Simon Nash. There were Nancy and Mrs Foley — But, no. She had forgotten that Nancy didn't live in. The maid used a bus to take her to and from Lynhaven where she lived with her aunt. Well then, there was Mrs Foley, and there were the two children. Mrs Foley slept in the room across the passage. The composer and the children had their bedrooms in the opposite wing of the house. Did Mrs Foley walk in her sleep? Yes, it could well be the cook she had heard, entering the room at the end of the passage. Kay had noticed the door twice, the first time when Simon Nash had escorted her up here, and of course again, much later, when she had turned in for the night. No one had shown her the room nor explained the purpose it fulfilled, and it hadn't crossed her mind to inquire or investigate.

Kay lay a long time listening, wondering if she would hear the person when he or she emerged from the room once more. She heard nothing else. Sleep claimed her at length and she slept without disturbance until morning.

Washed and dressed, Kay closed her bedroom door behind her and glanced up and down the passage before giving her attention to the door at the end of it. Plucking up her courage she approached the door and frowned when she saw no handle. Instead there was an aperture for a key, which indicated that it could be opened only by the use of a key. To test this she pressed lightly against the panelling without effect, then more heavily. The solid panelling refused to budge. Shrugging and endeavouring to shake off her vague fears, she continued to the staircase and the ground floor.

Nancy, whose full name was Nancy Gordon, was just making her entrance by the front door and greeted her with a cheery good-morning.

'Gosh, I'm frightfully late.' the girl said. 'You never can depend upon that darned bus. Some mornings it's five minutes early, when you have to gallop, at others it's ten minutes late. And what excuse do you think they give you?'

'Not a very satisfactory one, I dare say,' Kay smiled.

'None at all,' Nancy rejoined. 'You would think the passengers were doing the company a favour by using their buses at all.'

Directly breakfast was over, Simon Nash requested Kay to accompany him to his study, and wonderingly she went there with him. The study proved to be a small room off the library that he hadn't shown her yesterday, and was equipped with a desk on which were a telephone and portable typewriter, an easy chair and two straight-backed chairs. His den that he retired to when he wanted privacy? But no, the absence of a piano tended to disprove this. Of course there was the possibility that he had disposed of his piano when he decided that his career was behind him for ever.

The composer gave her no explanation. He asked Kay to be seated, offered her a cigarette and took one for himself. Then, taking the chair that stood behind the desk, he permitted a faint smile to hover on the stern features.

'No doubt you're asking yourself why I've asked you to join me here, Miss Ballard,' was his preamble. 'But as I thought we should be quite alone when I spoke to you about the children, I reasoned that this was the best place to come to.'

'I understand,' Kay replied, not really understanding him at all. Why was it necessary for privacy to speak of his children? She had gathered that it was his intention this morning to acquaint her of the exact nature of her duties concerning Diana and Nicholas, but surely he could have done this just as well in the library. Did he fear that someone would attempt to eavesdrop?

Something of her puzzlement must have been evident in her expression, for the other hurried on.

'This chiefly concerns Diane, Miss Ballard. I — oh, where the devil should I start!' he ended in frustration.

Kay's eyes widened. Diane! What was the matter with Diane? All sorts of awful possibilities crossed her mind during that moment of Simon Nash's hesitation. She had enough experience with children to make some wild guesses. Was the girl suffering from some physical illness that was not immediately apparent? Was she an epileptic?

The pain she read in the man's gaze urged her to try and make it easier for him to tell her.

'There is no need for any reluctance to explain, Mr Nash,' she said gently. 'Believe me, I know children. I've handled all kinds with all manner of illnesses . . . '

'Illness!' Simon Nash blurted in a voice that convinced Kay she had said the wrong thing. His attention diverted itself from the girl before him as he seemed to look inwards at his own thoughts. Then slowly he brought Kay into focus again. 'Yes,' he breathed, 'you could be right, Miss Ballard. I don't claim to be a physician or a psychiatrist. I had thought of it in terms of a phobia — '

'A phobia?' Kay echoed. 'What sort of phobia do you imagine your daughter is suffering from?'

'Her mother,' the composer said from a constricted throat. 'The accident she had. The accident that cost Caroline her life. Don't tell me you haven't heard of it. I'm sure you must have heard of it. Perhaps Murdock told you.'

'Yes,' Kay admitted, 'I did hear. I'm terribly sorry, Mr Nash. It must have been dreadful for you, for you and the children. But — but — ' Kay found she could not go on. How endeavour to cope with something that was beyond her grasp, outside her range of knowledge and comprehension?

'Please don't distress yourself,' Simon

Nash said. 'The last thing I wanted to do was resurrect the subject. But I must refer to it if I'm going to tell you about Diane.

'You see, she has this fixation, this phobia — call it what you will. In point of fact, Miss Ballard, those cliffs and the sea exert an unhealthy fascination over Diane. She cannot forget how her mother perished out there. She feels herself being drawn to the stretch of shoreline where she waited while Caroline was being brought in.

'At all times of the day, while she is at home on holiday from school, she goes there — down to the beach. To stand and stare.'

'But most children are fond of the sea,' Kay heard herself reasoning. 'And as for standing gazing out at the tumbling waves, well, I can do that for hours, and I'm sure I haven't got any sort of phobia. Being an island race, I dare say there is a sprinkling of sea water in the blood of most of us.'

A slight frown of annoyance greeted

this attempt at levity.

'I see what you mean, of course, Miss Ballard. I wish it could be explained away so easily. But it can't be. I know Diane, and I know what this feeling is that grips her. She does stand for lengthy periods staring at the waves, but it is always at the one spot she looks.'

'She was there on the beach on the day of the — the accident?'

'Yes, she was. I didn't learn until much later that she had been there.'

'So she saw the actual tragedy being enacted?' Kay asked hoarsely.

Simon Nash didn't answer her at once, but seemed to ponder over the question. At length a heavy sigh escaped him.

'Diane said that she was not a witness to the actual drowning. I hope to heaven that she wasn't.'

'So you don't really know?' Kay gasped. 'You think she may have been a witness to more than she was willing to admit?'

'Why do you say that, Miss Ballard?'

the composer demanded sharply.

Kay was thrown into total confusion. Her cheeks flamed with crimson. She realized what Simon Nash was thinking. The gossip, the ugly rumours that had circulated. Hastily she tried to mend the situation.

'For no particular reason, Mr Nash. Look,' she went on more firmly, 'if you would rather not discuss this any further, I shall forget it instantly.'

'Do forgive me,' her companion said contritely. 'I shouldn't have gone off the deep end. It is perfectly true that there is nothing but Diane's word for what she saw or did not see. In any case, it left its mark on my daughter, Miss Ballard. There is no denying the fascination the cliffs and the sea have for her. Did you hear her yesterday when I warned Nicky about going near the cliffs?'

'Yes, I did. She said she would watch him. Surely she wouldn't deliberately flirt with the danger that is there?'

'I don't know,' the composer replied

in a half groan. 'I'm not sure. I do want you to watch her, Miss Ballard. Now you can see my real reason for hiring a companion for the children in the summer months.'

'You want someone to protect Diane?' Kay murmured. She sensed that Simon Nash had not told her all the fears he harboured. There was much more to the problem than met the eye. Why was he reluctant to be completely truthful with her? Was there really some mystery surrounding the death of his wife? If there was, did his daughter Diane know more about the root of the mystery than she was willing to confess? And granting all that, what was the girl's reason for keeping what she knew to herself?

'You make it sound rather dramatic,' he rejoined, mouth quirking in the ghost of a smile. 'But in essence, that is what I require, Miss Ballard.'

'Why?' Kay asked with a bluntness that begged no apology.

'Why!' the other repeated. 'But I would have thought the answer to that was obvious, in the light of what I've told you. Because this unhealthy preoccupation with what is over and done with could be ruinous for Diane.'

'Mentally or physically? You see, Mr. Nash, I cannot help wondering if you fear more for Diane's reason than you do for the possibility of her physical involvement.'

'Physical involvement! Surely that is the nomenclature of the psychiatrist's consulting room. Don't tell me that you studied psychology also.'

'I did make a passing acquaintance of it,' Kay admitted, in perfect control of her emotions now. 'At the time I thought that a smattering of basic psychology would be a big help when I finally got in front of a class of school-children.'

'Was it?' The composer's features were deadpan just then and it was difficult to assess what his own thoughts were.

'Yes, it was. So I'm wondering if your

anxiety is more for the danger of Diane falling off the cliffs, or, somehow or other — ' In spite of her new determination, Kay found that she could not complete her statement. Simon Nash did so for her.

'Being drowned herself?' he finished flatly.

Kay's hands balled momentarily into hard knots. Her mouth went dry.

'It does sound rather fantastic, doesn't it?' she murmured.

Once again a heavy sigh escaped her companion's lips. He stubbed his cigarette into a tray on the desk and helped himself to a fresh one. He puffed it to life nervously. Then, turning again to the girl, he eyed her squarely.

'I've taken you into my confidence on this score, Miss Ballard. You might not believe that I've never discussed it with anyone else. It is my problem. You can very well suggest that the major portion of the problem has no existence outside of my imagination.'

'I wouldn't dream of suggesting

anything of the sort,' Kay replied. 'But what you have told me has roused my fundamental curiosity.'

'Why do I continue to live at Ashleigh if there is such a danger? Why don't I sell out the place and move to a different locality? Those are the questions you would like to put to me, Miss Ballard?'

'Yes. They are the obvious questions, aren't they? I could add another one. Why, if you retain these anxieties, don't you transmit them to an appropriate person, so that the subject can be dealt with professionally.'

'But, good lord, Diane isn't actually ill!'

Kay started to retort against this, but held the words in check with a supreme effort.

'I'm sorry, Mr Nash. I am not implying that she might be ill. With this accepted, your course should be perfectly clear to you.'

'Sell the house and clear out?'

'Why not? Do you have some personal reason for holding on to it?

You admitted yesterday that you have been tempted to move from Ashleigh. If I were in your shoes — sentimental reasons aside — I would certainly make that move for my daughter's sake.'

'You would, would you? But supposing your daughter didn't wish to have another home? Supposing, moreover, you had spent hours in endeavouring to get her around to your way of thinking, with negative results, how would you act then? Remember too that she isn't here for the whole of the year. Far from it. She's here only for a few weeks in the winter, spring and summer. She says she couldn't bear to come home to any other house. She thinks it would break her heart if she had to do so.'

Now it was Kay's turn to sigh. She did so involuntarily, illustrating how deeply she sympathized with the problem confronting the composer.

'Please have another cigarette,' he invited.

'Thank you, no. I rarely smoke much at any time.'

'Can you attempt to view this as I do, Miss Ballard? Can I expect you to do as I ask for the space of the next two months? At the end of that time your responsibility to Diane and Nicky will cease. I'll be enormously appreciative, and you will have the satisfaction of knowing you've been a great help to me.'

Kay hesitated before answering. Yes, there was an outlet for her if she wished to avail herself of it. She could refuse to remain at Ashleigh. The responsibility of constantly keeping Diane under surveillance might prove too much for her. Always she would live in the fear of something happening to the girl, when she would forever feel responsible, even though this mightn't be the case.

There was the other aspect to consider also — the mystery surrounding the death of the composer's wife. Despite any efforts she might exert to keep this from her thoughts, it would intrude inevitably. Had she really accomplished nothing but a leap from the frying pan of her own misery into the fire of Simon Nash's dilemma?

'Very well, Miss Ballard,' he said resignedly. 'I can see that the setup is anything but appealing to you. I don't blame you in the least for wanting to back out. What I should have done at the outset was seen that you were apprised of the complete picture. But you will admit that I made good this omission at the earliest opportunity.'

'You could always get another girl to fill my place. Indeed, Mr Murdock said there was a list of applicants that you could have chosen from.'

Simon Nash nodded.

'That is correct. I did get a list from Murdock. He forwarded each letter of application as it came to hand. It is true also that I chose the person I thought best fitted for the post.'

'If — if I left I would be letting you down . . . '

'You mustn't think of it in those terms, Miss Ballard. Well, if there is nothing more to be said — '

Suddenly Kay had a vision of the boy and the girl. Two wonderful children in this big house without a mother. That was really what the children required at this stage in their lives. If she took the opportunity to leave, she would always think of them, always wonder what had happened to them. Diane especially. She remembered how the girl had accepted her yesterday, how her face had lighted up on that instant of acceptance. Perhaps she could do more for Diane than had been done already. The challenge was infinitely greater than she had imagined it would be. But was that sufficient reason for putting her back to it? No, it wasn't.

'Well, Miss Ballard . . . '

'I have changed my mind, Mr Nash,' she said impulsively. 'If it is all the same with you, I would prefer to stay after all. Even as she spoke she had the sensation of having burned her bridges behind her.

6

Two days later Kay felt quite at home at Ashleigh.

There was little real work for her to do at the big house, her duties being exclusively centred on the two children. And, so far as Kay had experienced, Diane offered her no trouble at all. A pattern emerged that Kay recognized as an ideal one to follow. Around ten o'clock in the morning the three of them would go for a long walk that might take them some distance into the countryside, or the woods that lay to the south of the house and grounds. Also, it was usually Nicholas and not Diane who dictated the route they ought to follow. The boy was an inveterate explorer, and was never happier than when prying into some obscure byroad or plunging deep into the woods in the hope of seeing a fox or a badger. His sister seemed to tolerate him to a certain extent, and gained a certain amount of amusement from the wild flights of imagination he would indulge in.

'Nicky fancies himself as one of those pioneers you see in television westerns,' she said to Kay on the second of these excursions. 'Would you say he's typical of the children you are used to teaching back in Westcroft, Miss Ballard?'

Already Kay had coped with the surprise of hearing this girl talk as though they were equals. Being used as she was to dealing with girls of primary school age, she had found it necessary to make some slight adjustment when conversing with Diane. At the outset this had proved slightly difficult, but then, when she decided to accept Diane on the equal footing she not only desired but dictated, it became easier and infinitely refreshing.

Diane was possessed with a keen intelligence and a definite personality of her own. She was doing well at school, and so far had passed all her exams with flying colours. All in all, Kay found the true picture of Diane an entirely different one from that drawn by her father. This led her to wondering if Simon Nash was worrying unnecessarily about the girl's behaviour. Yet she decided to keep an open mind, believing that it would be wiser to wait and see before forming her own conclusions.

'Just about,' she said to Diane now with a smile. 'All boys of his age have the urge for adventure. You don't find his antics tiresome?'

'Not really. I find him very amusing. I suppose if we went to the same school, though, I'd get fed up with following him around. Look where he is now, Miss Ballard!'

At that moment Nicholas was well up in the branches of a chestnut tree, hanging on to a stout branch above his head and endeavouring to swing out to a neighbouring limb.

'Good heavens, he thinks he's Tarzan,'

Kay cried. 'Nicholas, please come out of there at once!'

'Don't worry, Miss Ballard,' the boy called laughingly. 'I know what I'm doing.'

'You don't, you know,' his sister retorted. 'And what did Daddy say about obeying Miss Ballard implicitly?'

'Miss Ballard won't tell on me.'

'Don't be so sure, my lad. Come along now and let's have you down here. At once!' Kay repeated in her classroom tone.

It was sufficient for Nicholas to descend from the tree with alacrity. Diane shielded a giggle as he did so.

'He obeyed you then and no mistake, Miss Ballard. Anyhow, we've seen enough of this old wood. Do you ever go swimming at all?'

'Yes, I do,' Kay replied, instinctively going on her guard. 'I'm rather fond of swimming actually.'

'That's super!' Diane exclaimed. 'Could we go swimming with you this afternoon? Oh, do say that we can, Miss Ballard.'

'All right,' Kay conceded reluctantly.

'But on the condition that I ask your father first of all, and that the suggestion meets with his approval. He is my boss, you understand.'

'I do understand. Gosh, why does father imagine I need a chaperone during the holidays? Oddly enough, I manage to exist quite well at school.'

'I'm sure you do.' Kay said somewhat primly.

'Oh, golly, now I've hurt your feelings, Miss Ballard! I didn't mean anything against you personally.'

'I'm sure you didn't,' Kay relented. 'And do remember, Diane, that your father has yours and your brother's best interests in the forefront of his mind. It's those cliffs at the back of the house he worries about mostly, I suppose. I don't blame him. If I were your parent I'd feel exactly the same.'

The blue eyes held hers for an instant, then Diane laughed and grasped Diane's hand impulsively.

'You'd make a wonderful mother, Miss Ballard.'

'What you're intent on doing is making me blush, young lady . . . Here we are, Nicholas. Had enough of imitating Tarzan for one morning?'

'Miss Ballard is going to take us swimming this afternoon, Nicky,' Diane announced then.

'Great!' Nicholas beamed. He had scratched the back of his left hand and there was grime on his face. Kay examined the scratch and told him to wipe his face with his handkerchief.

'Otherwise your father will think I'm aiding and abetting your jungle activities.'

When lunch was over Kay broached the subject of swimming with the children. Simon Nash's brow furrowed as he listened.

'I'm a reasonably strong swimmer,' she added. 'So I think I can keep the situation under control. Of course, if you have objections to the proposal — '

'No, not really, Miss Ballard. Yes, I do know the children love swimming. Both of them swim like fish. Actually I'm fond of an odd dip myself — '

'Join us then,' Kay invited.

Simon Nash laughed shortly and once again Kay was aware of the compelling quality of the gaze he bent on her.

'Thank you. Some other time, perhaps. How are you managing up till now with the pair of them?'

'They're no trouble at all,' Kay replied. 'As for Diane,' she added on a different note, 'she is a perfectly wonderful girl, so bright and intelligent. I'm continually reminding myself that she is only thirteen and not twenty-three.'

'Yes,' the composer smiled. 'Children seem to grow up more quickly these days. You wouldn't be much older than twenty-three, Miss Ballard.'

'Twenty-four actually. Almost twenty-five. I remember being eleven or twelve and thinking it would be centuries before I was eighteen. Now eighteen has come and gone and it seems as though only a short space has passed.

Age can be frightening, can't it?'

'I suppose it can be. The secret is to forget about the years, I would say. Some people find it hard to do. I'm thirty-six myself, and think about it now and again.'

'And feel twenty?' Kay urged jokingly.

'Good lord, no! Sometimes I feel a hundred. But there are compensations however. There are times when I feel innocent and childlike — usually in my creative moods. Those make up in part for the ugly days.'

Kay put her question that she had wished to put to Simon Nash since the first instant she had met him.

'Do you ever compose now, Mr Nash?'

The words had scarcely left her lips before she regretted uttering them. An expression of pain crossed the man's features like a dark, drifting shadow. He shook his head slowly.

It had been more of a snub than anything else, Kay thought afterwards.

But serve her right for daring to intrude on the composer's private preserve. His music was his own business, and if he had made up his mind never to compose again, then there was little that she could do about it.

The sand on the beach was like burnished gold under the hot afternoon sun. Kay and the children had donned bathing costumes in the house, and Kay and Diane wore beach-robes. Nicholas carried the towels and wanted to bound off in front of them.

'Take it easy, Nicky,' Kay warned him. 'It's a long drop down to the beach if you happened to fall.'

'I won't fall, Miss Ballard. I've been up and down dozens of times when there was nobody with me.'

'You tell terrible lies, Nicky,' his sister scolded. 'And you know very well you must do as Miss Ballard says.'

'Oh, all right!'

Steps led from the rear of the house to the beach. Her grandfather had had them put there, Diane explained. She had counted them and there were eighty-four of them.

'That's certainly a lot of steps.'

'Eighty-three,' Nicholas said. 'You always leave out the bottom one. It's a step too, you know.'

'That would be eighty-five, silly, not the other way round.'

'I meant to say eighty-five.'

'No, you didn't. You said eighty-four. Miss Ballard heard you as distinctly as I did.'

Nicholas glanced at Kay and dropped his eyes. He kicked a pebble into the cliffs with a scuffed sandal.

'I can swim further than you can, anyhow.'

'Now he is going to show off, Miss Ballard. How typical of your sex you are, Nicky! And you can't swim faster than I. I can swim rings round you. Dive rings round you.'

'We'll have a race,' Nicholas declared. 'You can't cheat when Miss Ballard is here.'

'No racing,' Kay said firmly. 'No

contests of skill or strength. Just a leisurely swim to enjoy ourselves. I'm quite certain you could swim the Channel if you had a mind to, Nicholas. But not today, if you please.'

'I'm sorry if it seemed as if we were fighting, Miss Ballard. We weren't really. But occasionally he makes me see red. Do you ever get angry, Miss Ballard?'

'Not often. Sometimes I do.'

'But not with your brother?'

'Definitely not with my brother. I don't have a brother, nor a sister, for that matter. I do have an aunt in Cornwall, though.'

'No mother or father either?' Diane persisted with her blue eyes searching Kay's face.

'My father died some years ago. My mother died only a few weeks ago.'

'I'm so sorry, Miss Ballard.'

'Thank you, Diane. Careful now, Nicky. We're almost at the bottom. Goodness! Hear those gulls scream and protest.'

'Do you know how my own mother died, Miss Ballard?'

'Mind that step, Diane. It's cracked in two places and you could trip easily. Whew! That is a long descent and no mistake.'

'Then you have heard how my mother died, Miss Ballard. You've decided that you mustn't talk about it. Perhaps my father ordered you not to discuss it with me.'

Nicholas had wriggled on past them to gain the beach and Kay reached out to grasp the younger girl's arm. The breeze blew strongly down here and the crashing of the waves against the cliffs added to the din. Blue eyes clashed challengingly with Kay's own.

'You mustn't talk in that fashion. Yes, I did hear about your mother's accident. It was an accident. Sad. Tragic. You mustn't go on thinking about it. You mustn't let yourself brood. Oh, Diane, my dear, the past is always behind us. There is a lesson it would pay you well to learn.'

Diane broke free and raced away from Kay, a slim, lithe figure on the threshold of young womanhood, leaving Kay with a vision of a haunted face, and eyes that would never forget what they had seen on the day of her mother's drowning.

Kay gasped as Diane continued her mad flight towards the lapping waves. She surged in against the pressing tide until her legs were covered, now her waist. Then she leant forward into the white-flecked breakers and struck out with what appeared to be nothing less than reckless abandon.

'See how Diane swims, Miss Ballard.'

'I see,' Kay replied from a tight throat. 'She is a strong swimmer, Nicky? I mean, really strong?'

'She's going out too far,' the boy declared and shielded his eyes from the sun with a scoop-shaped palm. 'She can't swim as well as she pretends. Want me to get her, Miss Ballard?'

'Good heavens, no, Nicky! One of

you is enough to cope with at the moment.'

The boy gave her an amused glance and tumbled into the waves, cutting out with the facility of a fish. Kay's gaze swung from him to his sister. Diane was nothing but a blob now on the dazzling surface of the sea. How the sun shone brightly! How that breeze whipped and keened!

'Come on, Miss Ballard!'

Diane's voice, amplified as the sea did with sound, floated crisply to Kay's ears. A hand was waved in invitation for Kay to join her. Or was it simply an extension of the challenge she had exhibited?

Nicholas was swimming inshore, as though somehow aware of the subtle strainings between his sister and the woman who was in charge of them, reluctant too to be drawn into any form of conflict he failed to comprehend.

Kay cast her robe aside and took to the water. The initial chill caress against her warm skin provided a tantalizing shock. She hurried on to gain her depth, then went into a smooth, sure crawl that had been practised to near perfection during her own schooldays.

The closer she drew to Diane the more effort the girl exerted to keep ahead of her. A laugh rang against her ears.

'Come along, Miss Ballard. You're lagging, you know.'

Not for long, Kay thought grimly and speeded up her crawl. Slowly but inexorably she overhauled the younger girl. Now she was a mere two yards behind her; now she had drawn level. From far behind them both, a boyish cheer greeted the performance.

Suddenly Diane stopped swimming and spun over on her back to float. Water dripped from her eyelashes and the contours of her face. Her eyes sparkled.

'You're quite good, Miss Ballard. Let's rest for a few minutes and then I'll race you back.'

'I didn't know you intended making a

contest out of it.'

'It's grand fun, isn't it?'

Was it, Kay wondered. Why did the girl imagine she had to compete with her on any level? Was she competing? Of course she was, if not with Kay then with something in herself that kept driving her. It was the moment when Kay realized how Simon Nash could be right and she wrong about his daughter.

'Are you ready to go?'

'If you are, Diane.'

'Then let's be off!'

Kay didn't spare herself on the return swim to the beach. Nicholas had emerged from the water and cheered them on.

'You're leading by a short head, Miss Ballard! Faster, and you'll beat her . . . '

Kay heard the laboured breathing of the girl, sensed the frantic energy that sent her pulsing through the water. A few moments later she was well in front of Diane. She peered behind her and saw those determined blue eyes. This would be another lesson for the younger girl to digest. If she wished to make a contest out of life, then she would be prepared for the elements involved to resist.

Suddenly Kay saw the situation in a different light. The shades were too subtle for immediate analysis. She slowed her pace deliberately, allowing her companion to draw level. Diane flashed a white-toothed smile and edged past. She reached the beach first and had flopped on the sand by the time Kay emerged. Kay flopped down beside her, her breast heaving.

'You should have kept going, Miss Ballard,' Nicholas told her. 'You were swimming very well.'

'Not well enough,' Kay panted. 'I felt like a tired horse must feel when it approaches the final hurdle. Congratulations, Diane.'

'To you too, Miss Ballard. I had to strain myself to the very limit. Golly, I'm going to lie here for an hour in the sunshine! It will take that long for me to get my breath back.'

They lay side by side while Nicholas continued with his swim. 'I'll race you both the next time,' he called.

'Why did you let me beat you, Miss Ballard?' Diane said presently, to the consternation of Kay.

'I let you beat me! Well, I like that. But I do welcome your modesty, Diane.'

'Rubbish,' the girl retorted. 'I couldn't have caught up on you if you hadn't allowed me to.'

'Good grief!' Kay laughed. 'You're talking the most awful nonsense. Very well! As Nicky says, there'll be a next time and another day. Then we'll see who's generous and who isn't'.

Propped on an elbow, Diane gave her a warm smile.

'I like you more than ever, Miss Ballard. You're a splendid sport and I'm not. Not really. I challenged you because I imagined you couldn't swim too well.'

'Why not? We don't have to take life so seriously. At least I don't, my dear girl. You'll find it makes things a lot easier in the long run.'

What a fraud she was, Kay reflected in the wake of her statement. Who took life more seriously these days than she? All the same, if a little bluff would achieve results with Diane, she saw no harm in perpetrating it.

They basked in the glorious sunshine for the better part of an hour before drawing on their beachrobes and starting back to the big house.

7

That night again Kay was roused from her sleep by a noise that had its origins outside the confines of her bedroom.

She had been dreaming of swimming in the sea with Diane and Nicholas, when Diane suddenly vanished and she and the boy began a frantic search for her. Then a cry from the distant cliffs showed them Diane standing there, laughing in a shrill voice and waving to them.

'I am not drowned,' she cried. 'I was never drowned at all. The man in the boat saved me!'

'*The man in the boat saved me!*'

The words persisted in ringing through Kay's mind as she raised herself up in bed and listened for a repetition of the noise. Had there been a noise, or was it the vividness of her dream that had brought her awake?

'Yes, I did hear something,' she mused softly. 'I'm a very light sleeper and it doesn't require much to make me stir. There it is again! A creaking or a squeaking sound . . . '

She heard what she fancied was a door lock being opened, then the door closed gently and there was silence.

Was that all? She had heard nothing more on the previous occasion. The floorboards had creaked, the door had opened and closed. Then nothing.

What did it mean? Twice during the course of these two days she had been on the verge of broaching the subject with Simon Nash, but both times something had held her back. Perhaps it was the fear that he would laugh at her. Perhaps it was the fear of having him believe that she was in reality a very nervous person. Nervous! Wasn't this house enough to test the nervous system of the strongest person? After this afternoon's incident on the beach she had been in a condition approaching on nervous exhaustion.

Kay willed herself to be calm and to contain her anxiety. It could be Mrs Foley on a nightly prowl. Or Simon Nash making his rounds of the entire house before turning in. Kay recalled that the time had been in the region of two o'clock when she'd been disturbed on her first night here. She looked at her wristwatch and noted that the present time was in fact just shortly after that hour.

She repressed a shudder, drawing the bedclothes closer about her. The next instant a scream rose to her lips, poised there and froze. Someone had struck the keyboard of a piano — one violent slap that sent out a harsh discord. Then there was nothing but silence. The sound had come from the room at the end of the passage.

Her heart thumping in her breast, Kay flung the bedclothes back and searched for her slippers with her feet. Next she switched on the bedside lamp and gathered up her dressing gown. With the garment on she moved to the bedroom door, opened it slowly and peered out. The passage was in darkness. The door at the end of the passage was closed. Not pausing to consider any possible outcome, she went on to the door of Mrs Foley's bedroom and rapped with her knuckles. She bit down hard on her underlip, hoping that whoever was in the room at the end of the passage would not hear. Who could be in there but Simon Nash? But perhaps not; it could be some prowler, a burglar.

The bedroom door opened and Mrs Foley, her hair neatly done up in curlers, peered sleepily at her. Sight of the wide eyes staring back at her caused the woman to gather her wits quickly enough.

'Miss Ballard — lass, what is wrong?' she gasped.

'Can — can I come in for a moment, Mrs Foley?'

'Of course you can come in, child.'

Entering, Kay closed the door behind her and leaned her back against it, glad of the support it offered.

'My, but you do look frightened, Miss Ballard. Here, sit down. I've got a little brandy that I keep handy for emergencies.'

Wordlessly, Kay waited until the brandy bottle was produced and a generous portion poured into a glass.

'There, drink it up and then tell me what is wrong?'

Kay swallowed obediently. The brandy was sharp in her throat but she swallowed the contents of the glass without pausing.

'Thank you, Mrs Foley. You must think I'm a dreadful baby.'

'I'll decide that later, Kay lass. Take this chair by my bed and tell me all about it. Something disturbed you?'

Kay nodded. Then, most of her courage returning in the comforting presence of the older woman, she blurted out her story.

'I heard it the very first night I arrived,' she explained. 'A noise. The floorboards outside my room creaking. Then a door opened and closed.

Tonight I heard the same thing, Mrs Foley. But tonight I heard much more . . . '

Kay's voice tailed off when she realized that the woman was frowning, and that moreover, she wasn't nearly so surprised as Kay imagined she should be.

'Go on, my dear. What else did you hear tonight?'

'A piano being played. Well, it wasn't being played exactly. There was just one violent discord, as though — as though someone had struck the notes with an open hand or a fist. He — he's in there now. He must be in there now — '

'Who, lass?'

For a second Kay was caught up in confusion.

'Why, I don't know. How can I know? I simply assumed it must be a man. Oh, I can see that you know more than I do, Mrs Foley. There is possibly a logical explanation for the whole occurrence.'

'Yes, there is,' the cook said at length. 'I'm sure that the last thing Mr Nash would wish would be to disturb you. I confess I don't hear a thing at night, even — even though I know he goes in there. Yes, it was Mr Nash you heard all right, Kay. You see, the room at the end of the passage is the one where he used to do all his composing. His piano and stuff are in there. His music, I suppose you would call it. Records. You know the kind of paraphernalia.'

Kay inclined her head slowly. Gradually the meaning of Simon Nash's visits to the room was being made known to her.

'You are saying in effect, Mrs Foley, that he goes along there with the intention of trying to take up where he left off. He hopes that by visiting the room the time may come when he can sit down at his piano and compose again.'

'I think you've hit it squarely on the head, my dear. I'm certain Mr Nash isn't aware of the frights he has given you. I could mention it to him tomorrow if you say the word. I wouldn't even say it was you who'd been disturbed. I could always tell him I heard the fuss myself.'

'No,' Kay protested at once. 'I wouldn't hear of it, Mrs Foley. Now that I know what it is, I won't be frightened.'

'Sure?' the elderly woman asked concernedly.

'Quite sure.' Kay mustered a smile. 'You're a darling, Mrs Foley. Thank you for babying me. I'm not usually so easily upset. But when you're in a strange house and all . . . '

'I understand.'

It appeared to Kay that the woman could have said more had she wanted to. Concerning the composer's wife and the boating accident that had caused her death? She couldn't be sure. But it was none of her affair.

'Well, thank you again, Mrs Foley. I'd better make my way to my own room.'

'You are welcome to stay for as long as you like.'

'I've made a nuisance of myself as it

is. No, I'll slip off. I hope you manage to get to sleep again.'

'I shall, never fear. Would you like another spot of brandy before you leave?'

'No, thanks, Mrs Foley. See you in the morning.'

Without more ado Kay left the cook's bedroom and sped across the dark passage-way to gain her own room once more. Just as she was on the point of entering, the door at the end of the passage swept open and a low-pitched voice sent a thrill racing over her spine.

'Why, Miss Ballard! Is anything the matter, Miss Ballard?'

'No, thank you,' Kay mumbled. 'I — I couldn't sleep and stepped out to see if it would help me relax.'

'And did it?'

'Yes, I think so.' He was framed in the doorway with a faint light glowing behind him, and Kay glimpsed the piano before pressing on into her room and closing the door firmly.

What an odd house, she thought

then. And what queer people who inhabited it!

Perhaps her estimation wasn't a fair one, but in her present mood she was prepared to judge solely on her experience up to the moment. The incident with Diane today had been hair-raising enough. At one stage she had feared that the girl would go too far out and would drown. The recollection sent more shudders running through her. She hastened back to bed, switched off the bedside lamp, and drew the clothes around her.

Why on earth did Simon Nash have to choose two o'clock in the mornings to visit his room or studio, or whatever he called it, in order to woo the inspiration that had apparently deserted him? Surely he could pick other times during the day just as well?

So far as Kay knew, he performed no duties about the house. She had noticed him wandering around the grounds alone, then again, she had seen him chatting with George Mallows, the gardener. If he had given up composing for good, was it his intention to remain idle for the rest of his life?

To Kay it seemed a terrible waste of time and energy. She was no fanatic where labour and time-saving were concerned, but what she could never abide was sheer idleness. It appeared so empty and aimless. Simon Nash didn't strike her as the lazy type. In fact, she could almost feel his energy and vitality in the air when she was close to him.

Perhaps he was biding his time, living in the hope that the day and the hour would come when once again he could sit down at the keyboard of his piano and compose more of those wonderful melodies. Kay fervently hoped that he might.

Kay remained awake for the better part of an hour, wondering if she would hear the piano once more. But Simon Nash hadn't been playing the piano — nor even attempting to play it. He had merely struck it in a gesture of what — frustration? Defeat? Outright fury at his inability to practice the art he had mastered so well?

At last she fell asleep and slept dreamlessly until morning.

Before breakfast Mrs Foley snatched a word with her, inquiring if she had recovered from the fright of last night.

'I was tempted to mention it to Mr Nash,' the cook said. 'But then I remembered that you didn't wish this and held my tongue.'

'I'm glad that you did. You see, as I was entering my own room after leaving you, the door at the end of the passage opened and Mr Nash spoke to me. I made the excuse that I was having difficulty sleeping. I'd hate having him imagine he was actually scaring the daylights out of me.'

The composer appeared more thoughtful than usual at the breakfast table. He was extremely courteous and polite with Kay, of course, but she sensed the air of detachment that enveloped him. It was as though his thoughts were somewhere other than in this room and with the people gathered about the table.

'Are we going to go swimming today, Miss Ballard?'

This from Nicholas as he helped himself to his bacon and eggs. As he spoke his sister shot him a keen glance, as if she expected him to describe yesterday's session to their father.

'Are we going swimming today,' she said.

'It's what I said, isn't it?' Nicholas returned.

'You didn't say that exactly, Nicky. We all heard you. You said, 'Are we going to go swimming today.' It isn't the best sort of English, as Miss Ballard will tell you.'

'You're smart, aren't you?' the boy grinned from a full mouth. 'You weren't so smart yesterday when Miss Ballard had to swim out after you and make you turn round. You might have swum to France or somewhere, if you hadn't drowned half way.'

'Nicholas!' his father said sharply.

'We can get along without this squabbling, young man.' His gaze moved to his daughter and Kay noticed how Diane paled. The girl's blue eyes flashed a signal of pleading.

Kay forced a smile that enveloped both the girl and the composer. 'Yes, you are exaggerating slightly, Nicholas,' she said. 'Diane and I had a swimming race. I believe she might cross the Channel if she had a mind to. I know I was hard pressed to keep up with her. And you're no mean swimmer yourself, Nicholas.'

A warm look of gratitude came from Diane before she bent her eyes to her plate. Nicholas rattled on on some other subject, but Kay only half-listened to him. She had seen alarm in Simon Nash's gaze for an instant. He feared for his daughter, Kay saw. But surely he didn't believe that Diane would deliberately put herself in danger?

'What shall we do this morning, Miss Ballard?' Diane said presently. 'Can we give the woods a pass, Nicky?'

'Perhaps I could make a suggestion, if I may,' Simon Nash interposed casually. 'Miss Ballard has seen little or nothing of Lyndale so far. Why don't you children treat her to a conducted tour? Would you care for it, Miss Ballard?'

'I would love to go to town,' Kay replied impulsively. 'If Diane and Nicholas are agreeable, of course.'

'A perfectly super idea!' Diane cried girlishly. 'Isn't it, Nicky?'

'Sounds great,' the boy responded. His eyes twinkled. 'I could show you where the amusement park is, Miss Ballard. There are dodgem cars and hoopla tables, and — '

'It's not what Miss Ballard has in mind, I'm sure,' his sister interrupted him. 'I can show you a really dolly boutique, Miss Ballard. Afterwards we could visit the art gallery. Well, being a teacher, you're bound to be interested in our local painters and sculptors.'

'Who wants to gape at a lot of old pictures?' Nicholas retorted scornfully. 'I bet our teacher would rather see amusement parks and things.'

Kay laughed merrily at them.

'I see we'll have to strike a compromise,' she announced. 'We'll visit all the places where Nicholas wishes to go, then the places where Diane prefers to go. Afterwards, if I may, I'll do a spot of window-shopping.'

'As you're our guest, Miss Ballard,' Simon Nash said with considered gravity, 'I imagine it's only fair that you should be permitted the initiative. Also, you are in charge of the expedition, and therefore hold the whip hand.'

'I wouldn't dream of going against Miss Ballard's wishes,' Diane said staunchly. 'Which car shall we use — yours, Miss Ballard?'

'Why not? I dare say the engine could do with a warm-up. Do you agree, Mr Nash?'

'Of course I agree. You two finish your breakfasts and then get dressed. You'd better get rid of those sandals, Nicky. Shoes would be more suitable for town.'

With the children temporarily in the charge of Nancy, Kay left the house to have a look at her car. The garage was a large one and she had parked it alongside the Rover. She was about to drive the car from the garage when she heard a footstep behind her and wheeled to see the composer.

'I've been thinking over what Nicky said about yesterday at the beach, Miss Ballard. Diane didn't really give you any trouble?'

'Trouble!' Kay echoed, feeling her cheeks growing hot. 'No, indeed. She did nothing of the sort. We simply all had a glorious swim, and as I said, Diane and I had a contest of swimming ability. She really does swim like a fish.'

It was difficult to know whether the man before her believed her completely. He changed the subject abruptly.

'About last night then . . . I imagine I disturbed you from your sleep. If I did, you have my profuse apologies.'

Kay was on the point of making a hasty denial. She hesitated briefly before inclining her head.

'You didn't actually disturb me. I did fancy I heard someone playing a piano, though.'

A grim smile flitted over his features.

'At two o'clock in the morning! You must think I'm crazy, I'm sure.'

'Not at all. I was slightly intrigued, I will admit.'

'Intrigued?' His eyebrows arched as he spoke. 'You no doubt wondered what I was up to. Well, I'll tell you, Miss Ballard. At that hour of night — or morning — I feel at my most creative. Would you believe that I used to do all my composing late at night? In fact I used to be at my piano into the early hours of the morning.'

'I can well understand that. Then — then you hope that one of these days — or nights rather — you'll suddenly find your old touch?'

'It's a vain hope, I'm afraid. I've dried up. Positively dried up. It does happen to creative people, you know.'

'Yes, I do know. But, Mr Nash, you

mustn't give up. You must keep on trying, no matter how long it takes you. I feel confident that the day will come when you will compose again.'

'Thank you, Miss Ballard,' he said gently. 'Thank you. Now,' he went on more briskly, 'can I help you with your car, drive it out of here perhaps?'

'I believe I can manage. If I bring the children home by lunch-time, will that suit you?'

'They're in your hands,' the other laughed. 'They trust you and your judgment implicitly, and so do I, I may add.'

'Thank you, Mr Nash.'

Ten minutes later Kay drove away from the big house, Diane on the front seat beside her and her brother chattering gaily in the back.

8

Seldom had Kay ever had a more enjoyable morning.

As a concession to Nicholas's youthful high spirits and enthusiasm, she voted for taking him to the amusement park first of all, and it was to the boy's credit that he objected to this, saying that Kay herself should have first preference.

'If you don't watch, you shall spoil him, Miss Ballard,' Diane announced in one of her more precocious outbursts.

'Oh, come, Diane. Surely not. And remember that if we pander to Master Nicholas's whims first of all, he will have to put up with ours later.'

Their excursion to the amusement park turned out to be a hilarious episode. Nicholas insisted that they each have a dodgem car and match their driving skills, and as it was ages since Kay had submitted herself to this form of exquisite torture, she found herself laughing frantically until she was hoarse. Driving an ordinary car on an ordinary road was infinitely preferable to the continuous bumping and whirling and crashing she was subjected to in the course of the succeeding minutes.

Diane and Nicholas were in high glee, crossing her way at every opportunity, vying with each other to block off her escape route when she reversed. At the end of the session she was quite breathless, but the boy's appetite had only been whetted.

'One more drive before we go,' he pleaded.

'Not for me, my lad,' Kay told him. 'You and Diane have another by all means. As far as I'm concerned, this is strictly a spectator sport.'

An hour was spent in the amusement park. It was sited within yards of the sea, and when they emerged they sat on the sea wall for a while, licking ice-cream cones and dangling their legs.

Kay was interested in the boats, mostly yachts, that flirted with the offshore breeze. She had never gone sailing in a yacht, and imagined it would be vastly exhilarating to do so. She mentioned this to Diane, who immediately suggested they hire a rowboat for a half-hour.

'There's a pier where you rent them over yonder,' she added. 'You can even hire a motorboat if you want to.'

'No thanks, Diane. I would prefer someone like your father to be in charge if we went boating.'

'Then I'll tell him,' the girl said. 'Father and mother used to do a lot of boating. They had their own cabin cruiser, you know.'

Kay swallowed tightly, realizing she had been thoughtless enough to choose an unsavoury topic.

'I didn't know they had. I dare say you and Nicky went out boating with them.'

'Oh, yes, we did. Very often during the summer. Even in the late autumn

Dad would take the boat out. We don't have it any more,' she concluded on a receding note. 'It was the boat which — '

'Yes, I know, sweetheart,' Kay broke in. 'Let's not talk about it. Boating accidents occur every day at this time of year, just as there are more accidents on the road. Well . . . what is the next item on the agenda? Bags I a spot of window-shopping. I saw a few large stores on the High Street. And then we must visit the art gallery. Shall we put it to the usual vote?' she smiled.

'There is no need to, Miss Ballard. I love looking round the shops myself. But please give the toy-shops a wide berth. Nicky's present fetish is model cars. He's got hordes of them, but he's always pestering Dad to buy him more.'

'That makes him more typical of contemporary boyhood than ever, my dear. You should see what my pupils bring into the classroom crammed in their pockets.'

At mid-morning, and before they had been to the art gallery, Kay took the children to a coffee shop where she had a cup of coffee while Diane and Nicholas had tea and sugary cakes. Both children were enjoying themselves enormously, but especially so was Nicholas, who on a couple of occasions in the midst of a crowd, had instinctively stretched out his hand for Kay to grasp. She had enclosed the small fingers in her own, at the same time feeling a smother of emotion in her breast. How often in the past had the boy performed so with his mother? Just then she deemed that, no matter what happened, she was glad she had consented to being the companion of the boy and the girl for these two months.

The local art gallery fascinated Kay, as it obviously did Diane also. It was patent that Nicholas shared little of their enthusiasm, but was content, nevertheless, to dog their footsteps from one section of the gallery to another.

At one stage the boy indicated a futuristic display of all the colours of the rainbow, which contributed to nothing more than an eye-dazzling conglomeration, in Kay's estimation.

'I could do as well as that myself,' he declared in a voice loud enough to reach the ears of other viewers and elicit sympathetic chuckles.

'No doubt you imagine that you could,' Kay agreed. 'Certainly there is a lot here that appears to be masquerading as art.'

'I wouldn't go so far, Miss Ballard,' Diane contributed with her air of wisdom. 'It is modern art after all, and some of it takes a reasonable amount of indulgence to come to grips with.'

'There I go right along with you, my dear! Indulgence is the word. But, honestly, I haven't the patience for it.'

An absorbing two hours was spent in the gallery, and finally the trio wended their way to the entrance door once more. In the street the sunshine was dazzling, and Kay blinked to clear her vision as a man's voice greeted her.

'Why, hello again, Miss Ballard.'

'Oh, Mr Manson!' Kay exclaimed. 'Fancy running into you like this,' she added to the grinning Bruce Manson.

'Fancy indeed! Well, it is a small world, they say, and getting smaller every day. Hello, my young friends,' he said to the two children. 'I see we're coming over highbrow all of a sudden. What were you doing in there — staring at those awful paintings and sculptures?' He shuddered in mock horror. 'Do please preserve me from museums and art galleries and all such follies! I bet it was at Diane's suggestion you went in there in the first place.'

'And what do you see wrong with modern art, Uncle Bruce?' the girl queried seriously. 'Can you explain what it is about it that disgruntles you?'

'Hey, you hold on with the strong terms, young lady. I didn't say I was disgruntled. I am not easily disgruntled, in fact. Where are you all off to now, by the way?' he wondered, his eyes admiringly on Kay.

'We'll have to make tracks for home

very soon,' Kay told him. 'I promised Mr Nash to be back around lunchtime.'

'But we've only met after ages! I've got a couple of hours to myself, to do with what I will. Don't you like your Uncle Bruce's company, kids?'

'Oh, yes!' they said in unison.

'Fine. Just fine. That settles it. Even if you decide to use your casting vote, Miss Ballard, you are hopelessly out-numbered.'

'But I don't understand — '

'I shall elucidate,' he said cheerfully. 'I am treating you all to a slap-up lunch at the Bluebird Restaurant along the way here. It's my favourite eating spot, and I'm sure it will be yours too when you've sampled the fare.'

'But — but I promised Mr Nash we'd be home for lunch, Mr Manson. I couldn't possibly — '

'Of course you could,' the young man broke in. 'There is a way around everything if only you apply yourself correctly. In this instance I propose to pop into a callbox, ring up dear old

Simon, and get his all-clear.'

'You think of everything, Mr Manson!'

'Just about,' he conceded. 'And my name is Bruce. I can call you Kay?'

'Yes, you can,' Kay replied with blushing cheeks.

There was a telephone kiosk nearby where Bruce Manson shut himself in and began making connection with Ashleigh. Kay's gaze shifted to the blue-eyed Diane who was studying her shrewdly.

'Do you like Uncle Bruce, Miss Ballard?' she asked disconcertingly. 'He's nice, isn't he?'

'I do rather like him,' Kay admitted. 'And he is nice.'

'I do hope Daddy allows us to stay in town and have lunch with him. Then he might spend an hour or so with us in town. Wouldn't that be super?'

'Super,' Kay agreed with her own inflection of meaning. She wheeled to the telephone kiosk as Bruce Manson emerged. He had a wide smile on his features, which proclaimed that Simon

Nash had given his consent.

'Your dear father gives us his blessing, my children. There is only one stipulation to be recognized. By you, Nicky, old sport, as it happens.'

'I haven't done anything, Uncle Bruce. Have I, Miss Ballard?'

'Don't be silly,' Diane told him. 'I'm sure I know what father is worried about. His over-eating. In plain language, Nicky, you mustn't make a pig of yourself.'

A wordy battle might have ensued had the children not been taken off to the restaurant directly. There Bruce Manson ordered a magnificent lunch which all four enjoyed to the full. With coffee at hand and cigarettes lit, Manson addressed himself to Kay, speaking in a voice that carried to her ears alone. The big dining-room of the restaurant was crowded just then, and there was a constant buzz of conversation. Diane was intent on the dresses worn by the young ladies in her vicinity, while Nicholas, a little tired from all the walking around, slumped back on his chair and rested.

'How are you finding Ashleigh after your initial few days at the place?'

'I'm thoroughly enjoying myself,' Kay declared, suspecting he was digging after something deeper.

'Simon is a rare bird, isn't he?' Manson said with a faint smile pulling at his lips. 'A trifle odd at times.'

'Odd?' Kay echoed and frowned at her coffee cup. 'If you don't mind, Bruce, I would rather not discuss Mr Nash. I never did believe in talking about people behind their backs.'

'Forgive me,' the other chuckled. 'I didn't mean to. I do see what you mean. All right then. Let's talk about something else. Let's talk about you, Kay.'

A short laugh escaped Kay. Already she was revising her former impression of this young man. He wasn't nearly as naive as he pretended to be. There was a depth to his nature that she found vaguely disturbing.

'There isn't much to divulge on that subject, I'm afraid,' she said 'Uninteresting background. Practically no history worth delving into. Being a school-teacher is quite dull actually, when viewed from a certain angle.'

'You don't find it dull?'

'Heavens, no! If I did I wouldn't stay in the profession for long. Security is a lot, but it isn't everything.'

'How true. Then you've no solid ties with the town you live in, apart from the school where you teach?'

He tried to make this sound casual, but Kay wasn't taken in by his smooth manner.

'What are ties really?' she rejoined cryptically. 'Something that binds you today, but non-existent tomorrow.'

Bruce Manson chuckled. On the first time he'd met Kay he'd noticed the lack of rings that could carry any significance. Yet he wondered if there wasn't some man in her background, wondered too how a girl as pretty as she was could escape being chased by a veritable horde of admirers.

'What do you do with yourself in the evenings?'

The question, spoken in the same low-pitched tone he was using, nevertheless sent a thrill coursing through Kay, and for an instant she avoided the young man's eyes.

'I lead a somewhat busy life, if you haven't noticed,' she replied, adopting an airiness to counteract his advances.

'Don't give me that, Miss Ballard. Simon might try to get water out of a stone, but he isn't the slave-driver you would have me believe.'

'Goodness, no, he isn't! He isn't a slave-driver by the wildest stretch of imagination.'

'We've sorted that much out at least,' Mason grinned. 'Let me frame my query in another way. What time in the evenings are you a free agent?'

'After about seven o'clock there isn't much doing,' Kay explained. 'But Mr Nash impressed on me that I mustn't feel married to my job. If I required a morning or afternoon free — or even a whole day for that matter — I have only to ask and it will be granted.'

'First-class!' Manson enthused. Evidently he thought he would have less trouble in winning Kay's favour than he had bargained on. 'Well then, what about tomorrow evening?' he said with fresh confidence.

Kay permitted her brows to arch slightly.

'What about tomorrow evening, Bruce?' she asked innocently.

'You could come out with me, couldn't you? If there is nothing to detain you . . .'

'Nothing but the inclination.'

'Inclination! The inclination for what?'

'To go out with a young man whom I scarcely know. I had a very strict upbringing, if the fact has escaped you.'

'Darn it, Kay, you're laughing at me.'

'No, I'm not,' she protested, yet unable to prevent a twinkle of mischief betraying itself in her eyes. 'Not that I don't appreciate your invitation, Bruce.

I do, naturally. But . . . Well, I like to have a quiet ramble in the evenings. I usually take a turn through the grounds, or go down to the beach and watch the waves coming in against the cliffs.'

'Sounds wildly exciting,' Manson said drily.

'Now you're angry with me, Bruce.'

'Of course I'm not. All right then, if you really must know, I am.' He relented and spread his hands on the table. 'How can a pretty girl like you be possessed of so much cunning?'

'Cunning?' Kay endeavoured to look stunned.

'Yes, cunning. I'm a cunning devil myself, and I ought to be able to recognize the quality in another person.'

They laughed together. Nicholas yawned and rubbed a knuckle on his eye. Diane had given up assessing the style exhibited by the young ladies at the adjoining tables, and was calmly considering Kay and Bruce Manson. For how long had she been listening in an their conversation? Kay wondered.

'What shall we do now?' Manson asked them briskly. 'A healthy stroll on the promenade in the sunshine?'

'I don't think Nicholas would appreciate it, Bruce,' Kay objected. 'He looks quite tired to me.'

'Oh, but I'm not tired, Miss Ballard,' the boy protested and pushed himself upright in his chair. 'Could we go down to the front and watch the yachts?'

'What have you got to say, princess?' Manson asked Diane. 'Would you care to go to the sea-front and see what's sailing?'

'Yes, I'd like that, Uncle Bruce. It's a change from being at home all the time.'

'What are we waiting for then?'

As they left the restaurant Kay puzzled over Diane's remark. According to her father, she was so much in love with Ashleigh that she couldn't bear to live anywhere else. Was this not the whole truth of the matter? Perhaps, if Simon Nash would be strictly honest with himself, he would admit it was he who was most strongly opposed to a change of home and scene. All the same, knowing what he did of his daughter's so-called phobia concerning the place where his wife had been drowned, would he not be inclined to put Diane's safety first and relegate the rest to its proper perspective?

The ensuing hour in the company of Bruce Manson proved a delightful diversion for Kay and the children, and when finally Kay said it was time she was taking the children home, he walked to the car park with them.

'When will you come visiting again, Uncle Bruce?' Diane asked him when she was settled on the front seat beside Kay.

'Soon enough, my beautiful one.' As he spoke his gaze rested, not on the younger girl he was addressing, but on Kay, who promptly began colouring. 'Watch how you drive,' he added before stepping clear.

'Don't worry, Bruce, I shall,' she

responded, starting the engine and accelerating out of the car park.

On the short drive home Diane was oddly silent for a brief spell. For Kay's part, she was thinking of the young man she had just left. There was no doubting that Bruce Manson was handsome and charming; yet there was a quality about him that Kay had found vaguely disturbing. It was the way he had spoken of Simon Nash that annoyed her. He seemed to treat Simon as something in the nature of an oddity. He was a flirt too, of course, and fancied he had a fascination for women.

'Uncle Bruce is rather nice, Miss Ballard, isn't he?' Diane said suddenly, breaking her short silence.

'Yes, he is,' Kay replied in a non-committal tone. 'I believe that I said as much before.'

'But you're not really fond of him, are you?'

'What!' Kay ejaculated before collecting her wits. 'There is a sparkling observation and no mistake. And what, pray, do you base that conclusion on?'

'Oh, I don't know. He looks at you in a certain manner, but it doesn't have much effect on you.'

'Well, I never! Now see here, Diane, please don't go building up a romance between me and your Uncle Bruce. Just because a gentleman is handsome and courteous, it doesn't necessarily follow that a girl must fall in love with him.'

'Just as you say, Miss Ballard.' Diane smiled and lapsed back into her silence.

Kay fell silent for the rest of the journey.

9

That evening there was another visitor to the big house, this time in the shape of Lorna Nash, the composer's sister.

The late afternoon had turned wet and the children sought their amusement indoors, leaving Kay at something of a loose end. Simon Nash had told her she might make use of the library whenever she wanted to, and that was where Kay was, browsing through a section of historical novels, when Lorna Nash arrived.

The girl, a slim fair, graceful creature, couldn't have looked less like a scientist to Kay's way of thinking, and when her brother had introduced her and they'd drunk a glass of sherry together, she chatted at some length about her work at the experimental laboratory in Lynhaven.

'We're an offshoot of a large chemical

firm, really, and dabble for the most part in commercial products. You must understand that before a patent medicine or a cosmetic or lipstick, or what have you, goes on the market, it is subjected to very stringent tests. That is where I come in mainly, and you wouldn't be far out if you called me something of a guinea pig.'

Lorna laughed when she said this, displaying beautiful even teeth. She was by no means a beautiful person, but was endowed with an attractiveness that Kay judged would make a big hit with a certain type of man.

While they talked the doorbell rang and the composer excused himself to go and answer it.

'Nancy has gone home and Mrs Foley is taking it easy by the television for an hour,' he explained. 'I can't for the life of me imagine who could be calling.'

The second visitor of the evening turned out to be a tall, huskily-built man of around Simon Nash's age. He was dark and tanned, and greeted Lorna as an old friend before turning to Kay.

'How do you do, Miss Ballard,' he grinned on being introduced as Hal Lambert. 'A school-teacher, eh? Well, I'd better watch my Ps and Qs while you're around. I confess I've never met a school-teacher since I was at school myself. Oh, happy days, when I didn't have a care in the world!'

'Get along with you, Hal,' Lorna joked. 'You're better off now than ever you were. Not for us ordinary mortals the benefit of long holidays in the sunshine in winter! You're right on top of the world, my lad, and you know it.'

'Right on top of the world! By golly, Simon, there's a first-rate title for you. Can't you just hear the tune running through your mind? Oh, you can't? Well, too bad. Seriously, Simon, old man, it's business — or the lack of it rather — that forces me to beard you in your den.'

'You're wasting your time, Hal,' the

composer returned with a touch of asperity. 'There's lots of young talent on the market at the present moment. Lots more only waiting for the right man to discover them.'

'Discoveries!' Lambert groaned, casting his eyes to the ceiling. 'Keep me a thousand miles away from new discoveries. Why, I could tell you a tale on that subject to end all tales . . . But no, I won't bore this charming company. But please, Simon, give me the benefit of your ear, like a good chap. Say thirty minutes or so.'

'It's useless, Hal.'

'How do you know it is? I've got an idea, I tell you. Would I come with my cap in my hand if I didn't have a bright idea.'

Plainly the conversation was taking an annoying turn for Simon Nash, and studying his clean-cut features, Kay had a glimpse of the inner torment triggered off by the appearance of his friend.

'All right, Hal,' he sighed. 'But we

can't talk here. Let's go through to my study.'

'Why not go straight upstairs to the music room?' the other suggested. 'I'm going to rouse you out of your enforced idleness if it's the last thing I do.'

'It isn't enforced idleness,' the composer almost shouted. He caught himself in time, ran his fingers through his hair and smiled apologetically at his sister and Kay. 'Do forgive me. Will you both excuse me for a little while?'

'Of course,' Lorna answered. 'Off you go and have a heart-to-heart chat with Hal. I'll stay and exchange experiences with Miss Ballard. But I do think we could move out of this dreary library, Kay. What about the living-room, and we'll fix ourselves cups of coffee?'

The two girls went through to the living-room and the kitchen. Lorna appeared to know where everything was kept, and Kay joined her in the kitchen as she switched on the percolator.

'Mrs Foley certainly keeps everything shipshape, doesn't she? I bet she'd have my whiskers if she suspected I was messing about in her preserve.'

'She is a darling really,' Kay smiled. 'The children treat her as they might a grandmother, and, honestly, I've come to look upon her as a sort of second mother.'

'She's a brick, no doubt, Kay. How are you making out with the children?'

'Oh, I adore them, Lorna. Nicky is so amusing, and Diane is the perfect little lady.'

'Yes, she is, but a trifle too grown up for her years, don't you think?'

'Perhaps. But children as a whole mature early these days. As if you're not familiar with what has become a well-worn cliche! That gentleman had something to do with Mr Nash's earlier career, I gathered?'

'Hal Lambert? Yes, indeed. Hal is Simon's agent. The best he ever had or is ever likely to have.'

'And his reason for calling is — is to try and encourage Mr Nash to begin composing again?'

'Correct, Kay. I don't know what has come over Simon. He's only in his mid-thirties, and yet he behaves as though he were an old greybeard with one foot in the grave.'

The vehemence that had entered Lorna's tone couldn't have escaped Kay, and it made her wonder. There had even been a tinge of bitterness in the way she spoke of her brother. At this stage Kay endeavoured to keep her curiosity in check, yet she couldn't help asking herself how much Lorna knew about the boating accident.

'Perhaps he never really got over his wife's tragic accident,' she hazarded tentatively.

'You can say that again, my dear. Ever since Caroline died he has retreated into a shell. He's only half a man since. Why, if you had known Simon before it happened, Kay, you wouldn't be able to recognize him now.'

'Has he changed so?'

'Inwardly. He used to be so gay, so witty. He would go around the house humming tunes, making fun with the children. I'm sure the children thought their father had died too and they'd got another model who merely looks like him.'

Kay thought this was a pretty awful thing to say. She held her tongue. Lorna appeared glad of the chance to talk.

'It's a good thing that children adapt easily,' the other girl continued after a brief pause. 'I'm sure you've noticed how they do.'

'Yes, I have.'

'And being a school-teacher, Kay, you would be reasonably well equipped with child psychology.'

Kay saw Lorna Nash would veer on to a different track if she didn't nudge her back to the one she was interested in.

'Reasonably well,' she agreed. 'I don't pose as an authority of any description, of course. Lorna, I'm sure that your brother must have been extremely fond of his wife. It was why he suffered so much when she died, I suppose.'

'Fond doesn't begin to describe what he felt for her,' the girl answered. 'Here is our coffee. Do you like it black or with cream?'

'Cream for me, please. If you're peckish you could find something in the larder to eat.'

'I'm not hungry,' was the reply. 'But I do like coffee. I drink far too much of the stuff, I'm sure. Cigarette to go with it?'

'Thank you.' Kay accepted the cigarette and coffee and waited to see if Lorna would wish to go back to the living-room.

'Let's stay here, shall we? It's a cosy little den. My, do you hear the rain coming down? It will help lay the dust, as my father used to say.'

Kay could certainly hear the rain. It seemed to be coming from the sky in solid sheets. When it slanted to beat in through a partly open window she rose quickly to close the window, then perched on a stool facing her companion.

'Where were we?' Lorna mused. 'Oh, yes, we were talking about dear Simon's devotion to Caroline. He loved her, Kay, as deeply as it is possible for a man to love a woman. In his sight she could make no fault, do no wrong. And all the time — ' Here the girl broke off to cast a sidelong glance at Kay. She shrugged and puffed alight the cigarette she held. 'Well, they do say that love is blind, don't they. I really cannot say, but perhaps you can?'

Kay repressed an involuntary shudder.

'I did think I was in love once. But I discovered that it wasn't the real thing.'

She spoke quickly, as though she now wished to keep all else that Lorna Nash might say at bay. There was something about the girl at that moment which fascinated and repelled her. What was she about to disclose concerning Caroline Nash?

'Good for you,' Lorna applauded, a faint smile curving the corners of her mouth. 'It could be that men are sillier than women, slower on the uptake where matters of the heart are involved. At any rate, Simon was either blind or didn't care what his wife got up to behind his back.'

For one tense moment Kay was convinced that she had not heard Simon's sister right, or, if she had, that the whole episode was taking place in a crazy dream and not in reality.

Lorna laughed softly at her reaction. Indeed, Kay had paled and her eyes held an expression of positive disbelief.

'I'm sorry, Miss Ballard,' Lorna said. 'I see that didn't go down too well with you. No wonder it didn't! When I first learned some of the facts myself, I was too stunned to work it out for myself. My initial idea was to go straight to Simon and let him know what his wife was up to — '

'That would have been wrong!' Kay cried impulsively.

'I know, I understood as much. And I had heard the old saw about two wrongs not making a right.'

'Oh, Lorna, this is none of my business,' Kay exclaimed then. 'I have no business listening to you talk about your brother and his wife. And you — you — '

'I should have more in me than to discuss his affairs? Isn't that what you mean?' Lorna heaved a heavy sigh and reached for her coffee cup. She drank and laid the cup aside. Her gaze moved back to Kay's features and remained there. 'The trouble is, Kay, that it isn't always easy doing what should be the proper thing to do. After all, we do have this quality called conscience. It might operate one way with me and in an entirely different fashion with you. Personally, I could never stand dishonesty and hypocrisy in human relationships. They are so alien to what life is all about. Life is truth, Kay. Life is sincerity. If we haven't got truth and sincerity, what have we got?'

A tremulous smile wavered on Kay's lips.

'So you are something of a philosopher as well as a scientist, Lorna,' she said in a desperate attempt to divert the conversation into a new channel. What the slim, graceful creature opposite her had just told her had proved shattering. Simon Nash's wife had been untrue to him! Here was one strand of the mystery being unravelled with a vengeance. What else might she learn from Lorna by the smallest encouragement? One half of Kay's mind wanted to hear Lorna out to the bitter end; the other wanted to turn a blind eye and a deaf ear, reject the whole thing as a tissue of fancy.

'I never considered myself in the role of philosopher,' the other girl responded. 'But I'm afraid I have shocked you, Kay, disillusioned you, even.'

'Disillusion?' Kay echoed, finishing off her coffee quickly. Her fingers trembled slightly as she held her cigarette for Lorna Nash's lighter.

'Yes. No doubt you formed your own

picture of Caroline from Simon's behaviour towards her memory. I dare say he has talked of his wife to you.'

'No . . . not really. It's a subject I'd hardly expect him to talk about. But, Lorna, are you saying that his wife was undeserving of his love? I find it somewhat difficult to swallow.'

'It is the truth, nevertheless. She was beautiful, of course. Have you ever seen a photograph of her? No, you mightn't have. After the so-called accident he systematically removed all the photographs that were around.'

The so-called accident! Here it was again. The hint of doubt. The hint that what had befallen Caroline Nash might not have been an accident at all, but —

Kay's thoughts refused to frame the remainder of the terrible alternative. There was only one alternative. No, she told herself, I must not think of it. I positively refuse to entertain the idea. The whole conception is too monstrous!

At the same time the question was

left hanging in the air. By ignoring it she would not lessen its significance. Surely it would be better to urge Lorna to come out with everything she knew or purported to know, and then argue the matter to the underlying fundamentals, showing the girl how loathsome and ridiculous her own beliefs were.

'I see I have shocked you again, Kay,' Simon's sister continued. 'But I'm not suggesting anything that wasn't whispered abroad when the boat caught fire. The story went that Caroline wasn't alone in the cabin cruiser. She often took it well offshore to bask in the sunshine and take the sea air. She fancied herself as a sailor, I believe. She would sunbathe, have a swim, then cruise to a different point along the coast.

'Simon was her companion occasionally. Now and then she took the children also. But, my dear . . . but! On this particular day Simon was busy upstairs in his workroom, the children had been left behind, all of which should have meant that Caroline was alone on the *Morning Glory* — the name of the boat incidentally.'

'Are you saying she wasn't alone?' Kay couldn't help asking, at the same time scarcely recognizing the hoarse croak that was her voice. Memory of the newspaper reports returned to her.

'No, she wasn't. A chap on a motorboat which was in the vicinity was certain that he saw another person on the deck of the *Morning Glory*. He couldn't say anything more definite. The police who investigated ruled out Simon and both of the children. Nobody saw a second person in the water. Therefore they concluded that the chap had been seeing things, or was of a mind to create mischief. The papers made the most of it.'

'Then surely that should have been enough to prove that Caroline was alone?' Kay argued tautly. 'Had there been someone else, and had that someone drowned also, then the body would have been found eventually.'

'I see your point, my dear. It's the point that was talked about and discussed for ages afterwards. However, there remains the unavoidable possibility that whoever was on the cruiser with Caroline, left immediately the boat caught fire.'

'Left!' Kay echoed in horror. 'Surely not. Are you suggesting that the man — if there was a man accompanying Mr Nash's wife — was able to swim back to the shore?'

'It wasn't all that far from the shore,' Lorna replied. 'Well, it was far enough for a poor swimmer or someone who couldn't swim at all. But for a strong swimmer there was little to hinder him reaching the shore a safe distance from the spot where, by that time, Diane happened to be standing.'

'I see,' Kay murmured in a stricken voice. 'This theory isn't entirely your own then, Lorna?'

'Not by a long shot. The story was told in the newspapers how the police tried to trace the missing man. At the outset Simon refused to consider the idea of Caroline being in the boat with another man. He had to face the possibility eventually. Still, I'm not sure what his own final conclusions comprised of. You must understand, Kay, that Caroline could have been deliberately and most foully murdered.'

For a long minute after the girl had ceased speaking Kay just sat there, rendered speechless by the shock of the hideous revelation. How she wished that Lorna had never mentioned the subject in the first place! But she had, and now she herself wondered what the real truth was. The voice of the other girl cut in on her frantic speculations.

'It could have happened that one of Caroline's men friends — a lover naturally, had tired of her and wished to throw her over. Caroline could have objected to the association being ended. She might have threatened her lover with disclosure of the whole affair to her husband, and the lover in turn — '

'But you don't know!' Kay cried out.

'You're simply guessing, Lorna, just as the rest of the rumour-mongers are guessing. And why, in any case, have you told me so much?'

'Why?' Lorna said reflectively. 'But why shouldn't you know, my dear? After all, you are in this house, working for my brother. It will help you to understand him, help you understand too why he broods so much, why he refuses to have anything more to do with his music.'

It was an explanation, of course, Kay thought. But she wished she had never heard of it, wished fervently that Simon's sister hadn't chosen this evening to visit.

Mercifully just then, the children discovered that their Aunt Lora was in the house, and swept into the kitchen like an enthusiastic hurricane.

10

'I'm afraid it was no good, Miss Ballard. Hal means nothing but the best, of course. But there you are, I have reached the end of the road as a composer, and there's nothing more to be said on the subject.'

Hal Lambert had long since left Ashleigh. Kay had seen him go and had noted how angry the big man was. The composer's sister had left also, and now the time was drawing to midnight. Mrs Foley had gone to her room, as had the children, and Kay herself had been turning from the library to gain the staircase when Simon Nash entered. He had begged her pardon, not realizing she was here. He was looking for a book to read, something light and not too demanding, he said. Caught off balance, Kay had allowed the first words that shaped themselves to trip off her tongue. She had asked Simon if he and his agent had produced anything worthwhile in the way of inspiration.

She should have taken his reply at his face value and gone on to her room, but a quality in the dark eyes struck some responsive chord in the heart of her being and urged her to say what she wouldn't have dared utter had she paused to consider.

'I'm sure you don't try hard enough.'

'What!' A laugh trembled from the throat of the man who confronted her, and it was obvious that he too was amazed at the boldness which had taken hold of her. But once Kay had taken the step she saw no acceptable reason for withdrawing or apologizing. She had simply said what she had decided was the truth much earlier. 'You surely must be joking, Miss Ballard. But no, by heavens! You are not joking, are you?'

'No, I'm not. But — No, I'd better not go on, Mr Nash. If I do, you will surely end up by telling me in the nicest possible manner that I ought to mind my own business.'

'Well, here's one for the book and no mistake! A primary school-teacher comes along — right out of the blue, practically, and tells me I'm not trying hard enough. Do you honestly suppose that — '

'Please, Mr Nash,' Kay broke in. 'If I said the wrong thing, then do forgive me. It is growing late and I must be getting off to bed.'

'No, Miss Ballard,' the other objected. 'That wouldn't be playing the game fairly. All games have rules, you know.'

'Where does fairness enter into it?' Kay gulped.

'I'll explain. You made a statement which you should be prepared to back up. You don't usually make statements without sufficient reason, I'm certain.

Kay felt her cheeks glowing hotly. What manner of little fool was she! Why didn't she have the sense to keep her mouth shut? It was evident that the composer had emerged from his session

181

with Hal Lambert in anything but a pleasant frame of mind, and here she was, doing nothing more constructive than adding fuel to the trouble which already beset him.

'No, I don't,' she stammered. 'All the same — '

'Good! Then let's stay here for a few minutes and give you the opportunity to enlarge.'

Before Kay could protest he had taken her arm and led her over to a chair. Kay plopped on it and Simon Nash then turned to the door of the library and closed it firmly.

He produced cigarettes from his jacket pocket and extended the case to her. Twin grooves etched the corners of his mouth.

'Go on and have one. I notice that you don't smoke a lot, Miss Ballard. Perhaps it might explain your clear-headed perceptiveness.'

Good lord, he was deliberately poking fun at her! No, the glint that shone in his eye just then was more an expression of gentle mockery than of anything else. Suddenly Kay felt herself rebelling. All right! If he really wanted her to be mercilessly frank with him, then she would be so.

'Would you care for a drink?' he said next.

'Thank you, no.'

'Very well.' He held his lighter for her cigarette, their eyes clashing briefly while Kay puffed it alight. Then, sinking into a chair opposite her, he made a gesture for her to continue speaking. 'I don't try hard enough,' he urged. 'Can we take it from there?'

During that moment of hesitation, Kay realized she was seeing another side of the man, what may have been a throwback to the days before he lost his wife. There was a recklessness stirring beneath the surface; a flamboyance of character that had been unnaturally repressed was struggling for expression. The revelation thrilled Kay in a strange fashion, and at the same time she was aware of the nervous tingling in the region of her spine. What was the real potential of Simon Nash, the true potential? Certainly he was a near-genius in the realm he was most at home in, but as a man and nothing else there were bound to be facets capable of sparkle and sympathy and warmth, and —

Here Kay clamped down on her flow of thinking. Her own imagination was threatening to take over and distort the facts and the bare essentials into the most unrealistic and romantic fancies. Yet, when she spoke there was no hint of rebellion in her tone, no trace of the aggressiveness she might have utilized as a shield against his mockery or a weapon of defence

'It is simply a matter of getting down to the basics, Mr Nash,' she heard herself saying. 'By which I mean that a person of your talent who has experienced what you have been through, should strip off the last vestige of cluttering and inhibiting negation, until there is nothing left but what you started out with.'

'I started out with an untuned piano in a third-rate dance band that called themselves the Nightlites. If my memory serves me right, we finished up at the end of the week with something like a fiver in each of our pockets. It wasn't a fortune exactly, but it wasn't bad for the period, and we didn't starve.

'Your perspicacity is astonishing, Miss Ballard. Your incisive thinking is almost frightening. Are you quite certain that you came to Ashleigh arrayed in your true colours? Personally, I see you in the role of psychiatrist rather than that of teacher to a classroom of infants. No, don't explode,' he hastened when Kay stormed to her feet and would have, on the very next instant, stormed on out of the library. 'I'm not making fun of you. I'm not trying to belittle you. You have turned your big gun on me, and it would be positively cowardly if you put it away and ran up any sort of white flag. You are talking from experience, are you not? You lost your mother recently, someone who was very dear to you. You have plumbed the depths of despair to their limit. But you didn't remain in those depths for long. Instead you made up your mind that you must pull yourself together. To do this it was necessary to divest yourself of your own negations, your own cluttering inhibitions. This you have endeavoured to do. You applied for a job. Positive! You acquired that job. Positive! You are now in the process of involving yourself in the lives of my children, and, judging by your success so far, that is positive with a plus sign appended.'

Kay slumped down on her chair again and gaped at him. It was all too crazy for words, she decided. She had surrendered to a foolish impulse in an endeavour to shake this man out of his apathy, and this was the result — a veritable avalanche of — what? — amusement, mockery, outright scorn perhaps?

If only she had gone straight to bed

in the first place . . .

A short laugh from Simon Nash added to her confusion. So he really did think her amusing! Well, at least that was something.

'Forgive me, Mr Nash,' she said hollowly. 'I'm sure I seemed to be talking in riddles. But my motives were genuine. You've summed up my own case pretty neatly. Immerse yourself in the problems of others and your own problems will fall away and be lost like raindrops in a river.' Kay's tone had taken on a tinge of bitterness, but still, she went on doggedly. 'Yes, I've discovered there is a certain amount of truth in that. And, as the remedy has proved successful to some degree for me, why should I not pass it on?'

'Why not indeed? So all I have to do is immerse myself in someone or something to the exclusion of everything else, and I'll find myself cured, or readjusted at the very least.'

'You *are* laughing at me, Mr Nash.'

Kay rose from her chair once more

and stubbed the cigarette she was smoking into an ashtray. At the moment she felt drained and frustrated and not a little angry at having made such a colossal fool of herself. The composer's next words caused her to stare at him.

'Far from it, Miss Ballard. On the contrary I have taken you seriously. Very seriously, in fact.'

'You mean — ' Kay gasped.

'I mean I am going to sample your homespun remedy. You could be right about me. Perhaps I was waiting for someone like you to come along and force me out of the lethargy that has poisoned my very system. And as my self-appointed teacher — '

'Oh, no!' Kay interrupted in turn, her cheeks fiery. 'I would never suggest being anything of the sort.'

'You refuse to help me?'

'I didn't say that.'

'Well, you'd better make up your mind, Miss Ballard. You either help me or you don't.'

'But what — what can I do? Oh, I

was only talking, Mr Nash. I didn't really intend to sound as I must have sounded.'

'Now you're implying that you lack the courage of your own convictions?'

'Good grief, Mr Nash! Why do you insist on twisting everything I say into something else entirely?'

'I'm sorry,' he murmured. 'Perhaps it is too late tonight to go into it any further. You are tired out, I'm sure. But we might take this up again tomorrow — carry on where we left off, as it were?'

Kay forced a wry smile.

'You're forgetting the children. Ready as I am to come to the aid of someone requiring my services, I must think of them first. And I am at your house in the capacity of children's companion, after all.'

'I appreciate all that. But we may snatch an hour off for another pep talk?'

'If you insist.'

'Then I shall insist. You see, Miss

Ballard, although I felt tonight that I would never compose another bar of music, Hal elicited a promise from me. He said the least I can do is try and try again.'

'I agree with what he said, of course. Can we be serious with each other for a moment, Mr Nash?'

'But my dear girl, I am serious. Believe me! This could be the last opportunity I'll ever have, the final chance to make good or bust. If Hal's brand of inspiration has failed to do the trick, yours might do much better.'

'I wouldn't go so far as claiming a magic touch that your agent is incapable of producing,' Kay told him. 'In fact, I can't really see what I could do, apart from urging you to do your best. Even then it would be most presumptuous of me to attempt anything of the sort.'

'You still think I'm joking about this, don't you?'

Actually Kay was at a loss as to what she should believe concerning his attitude. At the same time she must remember that Simon Nash, as a composer, was a pretty desperate creature. She was able to guess at something of the misery which any truly creative person would be prone to were he to discover that his art, and his ability to practice that art, had deserted him and might never be re-captured.

'No, I don't think you are joking,' she answered. 'I believe I can guess how you must feel — how you have felt since you left off composing. Any artist would suffer from the same frustration. But desperation does tend to drive one to clutching straws, Mr Nash,' she added with a weak smile. 'And this particular straw feels anything but adequate to cope.'

'Let fate decide, Miss Ballard, shall we?'

Kay inclined her head in acquiescence.

'Goodnight, Mr Nash.'

'Goodnight, Miss Ballard. I am deeply appreciative of the concern you have exhibited.'

On that note Kay took her leave of

the composer, hastening into the hall and on to the stairway that would lead her to her room. Inside her bedroom she stood at the closed door for a moment, her thoughts in a whirl of utter confusion. She had the feeling of having emerged from a strange dream. But no, she hadn't emerged at all. She was still enmeshed in the dream. It was a strange, uneasy sensation that was going to prove difficult to shake off.

Heaving a heavy sigh, she slumped down on the stool at the dressing table. Her features were pale and drawn, she saw, and no wonder they were! Her eyes seemed large and staring. If a few days at Ashleigh could do this to her, then what transformation would two whole months bring?

'But I don't have to remain here against my will,' she consoled herself. 'I haven't signed any contract nor committed myself irrevocably. First thing in the morning if I wish, I can pack my cases and walk out of here.'

She had been getting along fine until

tonight, she reflected. Until Simon Nash's sister turned up and went over that awful tale. Surely there was no solid foundation for the rumours which Lorna had insisted on reciting? The girl was a nice enough person, and Kay was sure that the last thing on her mind had been any desire to worry her or make her stay unpleasant.

'But supposing — just supposing — there was someone in the cabin cruiser that day with Caroline, and supposing she was deliberately murdered . . . Does Simon know that? Does he share the suspicions of his sister?'

It was a long time before sleep came to Kay that night, but mercifully her sleep was undisturbed and dreamless.

11

As Kay had suspected, once Bruce Manson was taken by a pretty face it wasn't so easy to keep dodging him. On the very next day at lunch-time — just as Kay and the two children returned from a long walk on the beach — he made a telephone call to the house. It was Nancy who anwered the telephone and then summoned Kay to speak with the young man.

'Bruce Manson?' Kay echoed, taken by surprise and noting the mischievous twinkle in the eye of the maid. 'I wonder what on earth he could want with me . . . Are you sure he asked for me by name, Nancy?'

'There is no doubt that he did, Miss Ballard,' the girl smiled and left Kay alone at the telephone.

'Ah, hello there, Miss Ballard!' Manson greeted her breezily. 'I don't suppose you expected me to get in touch again so soon. To be ruthlessly honest, Kay,' the other continued before she could get a word in, 'I'm having the devil of a job getting you out of my mind.'

Kay stifled a giggle of amusement. She had seen the smooth, the gay, and the innocent guises that Bruce could adopt at will. Now he was playing the role of admirer for all he was worth and hoping she would snatch at the bait he offered. Kay had seen enough of his type not to be fooled in any fashion by Manson's personification of it. But if he had a mind to play games with her, then she would pretend to let him dictate the rules.

'That sounds rather alarming, Bruce,' she answered. 'Could I suggest something that might permit you a little peace.'

'That sounds suspiciously like a sugar-coated pill, Kay, with a really nasty substance beneath the sugar. But if it humours you I'll buy it. What's the cure?'

'It's a simple remedy actually, Bruce. You just exercise the minimum of will-power and force yourself to think of something different. Work is an excellent remedy also. I know that I find it wonderfully engrossing and stimulating.'

'Ugh!' Manson said. 'I don't feel much better yet, Kay.'

'I dare say it was the mention of work.'

'Of course it was. I'm bone-lazy at heart. I would make a first-class millionaire. Well, you do hear of these fellows who are absolutely loaded with money, but who contrive to be as miserable as sin. Now, I'd be the very opposite. A million or two would suit me. I'm the ideal sort for loafing in the sun, with a fat cigar in my mouth and a double scotch and soda at my elbow.'

'Bruce, it all sounds horribly deca-dent. And I'm not in the least sure it would become you . . . Look, I'll have to dash if I'm to have my lunch. We can discuss millionaires and fat cigars some other time.'

'Oh, just a minute now, Kay,' Manson protested. 'You almost caused me to forget what I intended to say to you in the first place.'

'But you did say it. You aren't feeling so good. And really, Bruce, if you aren't, shouldn't you get in touch with your doctor?'

Kay hung up on that note, certain that Manson would be furious at her action. She wore the traces of amusement as she sat down to lunch with the children and their father.

'I believe you had a long walk on the beach, Miss Ballard.'

'Yes, we had.' Kay told Simon Nash. 'The seaside is certainly marvellous at this time of year.'

'You didn't have bad news, I trust,' he said in the next breath.

'Bad news?' Kay repeated blankly before realizing what it was the composer referred to. 'Oh, the telephone call! It was Bruce Manson, actually,' she confessed and blushed.

'Indeed!' Simon Nash murmured while his eyebrows rose. 'So my prediction is coming true after all.'

This was the only comment he ventured to make, and Kay, not wishing to encourage any further talk regarding Manson, was quite happy to let the subject lapse. Had the children not been present however, she would have explained to the composer in no uncertain terms that his cousin it was who was grasping the initiative. The opportunity to do this did not arise and Kay was forced to swallow her frustration.

The meal was scarcely over before Nancy came to summon Kay to the telephone again.

'You must be joking, Nancy,' Kay laughed shortly. 'Who is asking for me this time?'

'Mr Manson,' the maid informed her delightedly.

'You'd better tell him that I've gone out, Nancy.'

'Tell him a lie!' the girl cried in

simulated amazement. 'But you haven't gone out, Miss Ballard.'

'Talk about a conspiracy!' Kay grumbled on her way to speak to Bruce Manson. 'Now see here, Bruce,' she said to him a moment later, 'by ringing me in this manner you are causing me no end of embarrassment — '

'Oh, do come off it, Kay! Are you saying that Simon objects to my having a chat with you during your working hours?'

'I'm saying nothing of the kind. But it is embarrassing all the same, Bruce. Now do tell me what you want.'

'Very well, teacher, I shall. I want a date with you.'

'Yes! I thought you might be leading up to something of the sort. Well, it isn't possible, kind sir. I'm sorry . . . '

'Not nearly as sorry as you'll be when I've rung you up a dozen times between now and the evening,' he returned blithely.

'You wouldn't, Bruce!'

'I would, you know.'

'But — but that's nothing short of blackmail.'

'Is that what they call it? In any case, Kay, it's what you're going to have if you don't concede to my demands with the utmost alacrity.'

'I could have you shot,' Kay stated. 'I saw a film one time where a character behaved as you intend to behave. He was disposed of in the best possible manner.'

'No doubt,' Manson chuckled. 'But not before the final reel of the drama. In between, I bet, he had one whale of a time with the lady in question. Besides, you would never hire a gunman to shoot me. You haven't got the heart for it.'

'I suppose you're right.' Kay heaved a sigh. 'What form does this blackmail propose to take?'

'The mildest form there is. A date, dear lady. Tonight if possible.'

'If I say no?'

'Then I'm afraid the old telephone will buzz quite frequently between now and nightfall.' Manson threatened. 'By golly, I might not stop there! I could pester you at all hours of the night also. I could have a dilly of a time to myself.'

'You frightful sadist, Bruce! All right, I know when I'm beaten. What time will you arrive to carry me off to your lair in the mountains?'

'You really mean it?' the other cried boyishly.

'Well, don't you?' Kay cried.

'Would seven o'clock suit you?'

'Yes, I'm sure it would. I have my own car, as you know. I could meet you in Lynhaven . . . '

'You'll do no such thing, teacher. I'll call for you in my own chariot. You'll know I've arrived when you hear my trumpet of triumph blowing at the door.'

'Try it and Mr Nash will have your life,' Kay laughed.

'Until seven o'clock then. You won't change your mind at the moment of truth?'

'Not really, Bruce. Goodbye.'

'So he's on with you again,' a voice said at Kay's back. She wheeled sharply to see Simon Nash smiling at her. 'Do forgive me, Miss Ballard. I didn't intend to startle you. It was Bruce again, wasn't it?'

'Yes, it was,' Kay answered with a shrug of her slim shoulders. 'And as you hinted, Mr Nash, he's a difficult young man to shake off.'

'Just as I knew! Show him a pretty face and it turns his head. Not that I don't have some sympathy with him, you must understand.'

'Thank you,' Kay said, blushing to the roots. It was the first time that the composer had paid her the sort of compliment a pretty girl expects from a handsome man. 'He asked me to go out with him this evening. Should I bring a shotgun along, do you think?'

Simon Nash joined in her laugh briefly. He sobered just as easily as he had unbent.

'You haven't forgotten what we talked about last night, Miss Ballard?' he said in a measured tone.

Kay shook her head slowly. Last night seemed a dim memory to her now. This morning she had awakened with a more balanced perspective, determined to forget the visit of Lorna Nash and all the girl had said concerning her dead sister-in-law. The early outing with Diane and Nicholas had contributed vastly to the new outlook she wished to cultivate. Of course she had not forgotten the conversation she had had with the composer. Yet she wished it had never occurred. She had acted impulsively last night, spoken impulsively. She had harboured the hope that Simon Nash would decide to put the incident behind him.

Apparently this was not to be so.

'No, I haven't forgotten,' she answered now. 'But on reflection, Mr Nash, I fail to see how I could offer anything constructive.'

'You wish to back out?' he asked gently.

'Good heavens, no! Honestly, I would do anything in my power to help you resume your interest in your music.'

'Thank you, Miss Ballard. We shall take it up later then? I trust you have a nice time with Bruce. I don't imagine you will really need a shotgun,' he added smilingly.

He was turning to leave her when Kay yielded to yet another wild impulse.

'Mr Nash, listen . . . You don't go out much yourself, I see. Why not break with the tradition you have established, as it were, and come out this evening with Bruce and me?'

The look of surprise which flitted across the face of the composer caused Kay to catch her breath. Then for an instant it seemed he would accept her proposal. Finally he made a shrugging motion with his shoulders.

'Thank you for the thought. I'm not sure whether it was motivated by your desire for protection, or was purely unselfish. In any case, my cousin would most definitely miss the point.'

He left Kay with a high colour in her cheeks. For the briefest of moments then she had detected some manner of spark coming to life in him. It had not lasted for long enough to permit analysis, but it had shown Kay that he was capable of responding. Capable of responding to what — kindness? Sympathy? The company of another woman?

She battled with the surge of feeling that swept over her. Yes, she would help him to regain his inspiration and the will to carry on with his career. Exactly how this could be accomplished, or how she might contribute to its accomplishment, was beyond the scope of her comprehension, just then at any rate.

Out of doors she discovered Nicholas careering round the grounds on his bicycle. When she inquired where his sister was, the boy was unable to tell her.

'But she isn't in the house,' Kay argued. 'Are you sure she isn't riding her bicycle also, Nicky?'

'I don't know, Miss Ballard. The last time I saw her she was off through the trees yonder.'

Good heavens, Kay thought in alarm. Surely the girl hadn't gone off to the beach by herself! She was walking towards the fringe of the grounds to gain the steps leading to the beach when Nicholas darted in her wake on his bicycle.

'Are you going swimming, Miss Ballard? Can I go with you?'

'No, Nicky. You remain where you are for the present. I'm going to see what your sister is up to.'

'I bet she's down there looking at the sea,' the boy said. 'She sneaks away often to do that.'

Hurrying her step, Kay continued to the cliffs. When she arrived at the top of the flight of stone steps she halted to gaze beneath her. Yes, there was Diane sure enough. She was sitting on a boulder on the sand, her cheeks cupped in her hands, and gazing out to sea.

'Diane!' Kay called. 'Can you hear me?'

A stiff breeze was blowing as it usually was on the seafront, and this together with the muted roaring of the breakers coming in to lap the base of the cliffs, effectively blotted out her voice before it could reach the girl's ears.

Without further ado Kay began to descend the steps. She would have to talk with Diane, she decided. She would have to impress on her the necessity of staying within her range. At the same time Kay experienced a flood of emotion. How lonesome the child — well, she wasn't much more than a child for all of her sophistication and precociousness — must feel without her mother. In the wake of this thought another one occurred to Kay. It hadn't been yesterday when Diane lost her mother. It had been almost three years ago, if her calculation was right. So that

Diane should have made some effort to pull herself together and forget the tragedy that was past.

Even when Kay had gained the beach, the girl continued to sit where the waves lapped in, oblivious of all else around her. What was she thinking of at that moment — the burning cabin-cruiser and her mother at the mercy of the sea? Whatever it was, it was a distinctly unhealthy pastime and should be discouraged.

'Didn't you hear me call to you, Diane?'

At so close range the girl could not fail to hear Kay now; she turned her head swiftly, surprise crossing her features to be followed closely by annoyance. Then she had command of herself and smiled as Kay approached.

'Why, hello, Miss Ballard! You gave me a start then. It's impossible to hear anything but the sea when you're so near to it.'

If she imagined she could wriggle out of this, Kay had other ideas.

'I don't like you running off on your own, Diane,' she said in a stern voice. 'When I asked Nicky where you were, he couldn't tell me. It gave me quite a fright, I might tell you.'

'Oh, I'm sorry, Miss Ballard. But there's no need to worry about me. Really there isn't. I'm old enough to take care of myself. Daddy worries too when I go for a walk by myself.'

'Shouldn't you remain within earshot of the house in that case? If something should happen to you, it would be all over before anyone could get down here to help you.'

'But nothing can happen to me, Miss Ballard. I can guess what Daddy fears,' she went on swiftly. 'Knowing how Mummy was drowned out there, he is in terror that I might drown also, or fall from the cliffs, or something equally unlikely and silly.'

For a moment Kay was too stunned to do other than gape at the girl. Finally she found her voice.

'Then — then you realize how your

father worries, Diane?'

'Yes, I do. I didn't really understand at first. He was always having some-body spy on me during the school holidays. If it wasn't Nancy, it would be Mr Mallows. This year he decided to hire a companion for us — ostensibly, that is. Oh, don't think that I resent the precautions my father takes, Miss Ballard. I don't. But being followed around can be tiresome, you must admit.'

Her logic was too profound to be denied.

'Yes, I — I suppose I can see your point, Diane. But you do see your father's as well?'

'Of course I do. Won't you sit here a while with me and watch the sea?'

'Why not?' Kay responded with more cheerfulness than she felt. The girl made room for her on the flat rock and Kay sat down beside her.

'Smoke a cigarette if you want to, Miss Ballard. You do smoke occasion-ally, don't you?'

'Just occasionally. I haven't any cigarettes with me. I don't really want to smoke anyhow . . . Diane, tell me, what do you think of when you sit here in this fashion?'

The girl flashed her a bright smile before realizing how serious her companion's mood was just then.

'Goodness, I don't know. I could hardly tell you. Lots of things, I suppose. How vast the oceans are. The lands that lie beyond the horizon.' She broke off and laughed briefly. 'I dare say I have a romantic turn of mind.'

'And that is all you think of?'

'What else, Miss Ballard? Oh, I understand! You imagine I am pining for my mother, that I've got some morbid curiosity — a fascination perhaps — for the place where my mother was drowned.'

Kay's heart skipped a beat.

'And you haven't?' she asked softly.

'No, I haven't, Miss Ballard. Honestly. After all, I'm old enough to cope with the realities of life.'

'Of course, my dear, of course!' Having been successful so far. Kay wondered if she should ask another question — the question she was so eager to ask this girl. 'You probably read — or heard of — some of the rumours that were rife following your mother's terrible accident?'

'Yes, I did,' Diane answered immediately. 'There was supposed to have been someone in the *Morning Glory* with her when it caught fire and sank. Well, I arrived on the beach shortly after the boat caught fire, and I certainly didn't see anyone.'

'They were nothing but rumours, Diane.'

'Miss Ballard, you are crying — '

'No, I'm not! Oh, you dear, dear child . . . ' Yielding to an impulse, Kay put her arm about the girl's shoulder and hugged her tightly. 'Well, I'm sure you've communed enough for one day. Shall we go and find Master Nicholas? And, Diane, I must tell you, your Uncle Bruce has asked me to go out with him this evening.'

'Super, Miss Ballard! Perhaps you won't have to leave us again after all. You might finish up marrying Uncle Bruce and staying on at Lynhaven.'

'Heaven forbid,' Kay laughed. 'How could I ever cope with such a man?'

Hand in hand they made their way along the sandy shore to the stone steps, Kay's heart immeasurably lighter.

12

Bruce Manson arrived at Ashleigh for Kay on the stroke of seven. Kay had stayed out later than she'd planned with the children, and, as a result, wasn't quite ready at the appointed moment. It was Nancy who answered the door, and when she'd let the young man in she called upstairs to Kay.

'Mr Manson, Miss Ballard!'

'Won't be a minute.'

Nancy should have left earlier to catch her bus into town, but Kay had told her she might as well take a lift with her and Bruce. She was sure that Bruce would leave the girl off at her own home.

While he waited for Kay, Manson chatted with his cousin in the library, then, as Kay swept downstairs, he met her in the hall and led her on to the door.

'Oh, wait, Bruce. Where is Nancy? I promised we would drop her off at her house.'

'Here I am, Miss Ballard,' Nancy announced just then. 'I hope I won't be putting you out, Mr Manson.'

'Not a chance,' Bruce grinned at her. 'Shall we go then, ladies?'

At the doorway Kay remembered that she hadn't spoken to Simon Nash regarding the time of her return. Manson frowned slightly when he saw her hesitation.

'Your lord and master knows you are leaving.'

'I should have stated a time when I'll get back.'

'And spoil him?' Manson chuckled. 'You've got a lot to learn, teacher, even if you don't realize you have.'

Bruce's car was a two-year old model which came from the same stable as a host of racing cars. With the two girls seated, he clambered behind the wheel and shot away from the house.

'Good heavens!' Nancy panted. 'I

might have been safer taking my bus after all.'

'Yes,' Kay replied. 'And I might have been safer if I'd remained at home.'

It was plain that the young man was intent on displaying his skill with the car. When he approached the outskirts of Lynhaven however, he slowed to the required speed limit. Nancy Gordon lived in a semi-detached bungalow with her aunt, and they laid her down at the door, said goodbye and drove off to the centre of town.

'Where do we go from here?' Bruce Manson asked then.

'You don't have your plans cut and dried?' Kay wondered in mock amazement. 'I'd imagined you'd have everything arranged to the last detail. Well, it is a wonderful evening . . .'

'Too good to be spent indoors, you'll agree?'

'I'd much rather stay outdoors,' Kay smiled.

'Then I'll make a suggestion,' Manson

said. 'We'll go for a drive, a long, leisurely drive, when I'll show you part of our attractive coastline. How does that sound?'

'Sounds all right to me, Bruce. But on one condition.'

'Which is?' he nudged with blue eyes glinting.

'That you drive carefully and within a reasonable speed limit. I'm very nervous in a car that I don't happen to be driving.'

'Isn't that a coincidence? I'm never at ease on the passenger seat. I find myself tense all the time. You know, I grit my teeth and clench my hands, and get into a fine old sweat. With the wheel in my own hands I feel differently.'

'I've noticed,' Kay smiled. 'Off we go then.'

The coastline was a revelation to Kay. For a stretch of almost fifteen miles the road that Bruce took ran parallel with the sea, and on a gloriously sunny evening such as it was, the view was breathtaking. She said as much to her companion.

'It takes the sunshine,' Bruce observed. 'On a dull day or a wet day the effect is the complete opposite. It is thoroughly miserable and depressing. I must admit,' he added with a laugh, 'that it's ages since I've been on this road, wet or dry.'

'Fraud!'

'Not really. You're a stranger in our midst. As well as being a stranger, you're also a school-teacher, which means you're bound to have a smatter-ing of culture — '

'That sounds almost as depressing as a wet day!' Kay groaned. 'What is culture?'

'Don't ask me, Kay. If you don't know, we're lost. I write silly slogans and things that people buy to advertise their wares. It's all very commercial and all basically phoney. To get back to you, I thought you would enjoy feasting your eyes on the wonders of nature. Are you saying that you don't?'

'Of course not,' Kay said quickly. 'But don't tag any labels on to me, please. I detest labels.'

'Me too,' Manson grinned. 'We seem to share a lot of tastes, don't we? Look, here is a quiet spot where we can halt and find out just how much we really have in common.'

The spot he indicated was a lay-by, bordered by a white railing, beyond which was a winding path through the rocks to the beach. Theirs was the only car in evidence, and when Bruce halted Kay alighted and went to lean over the fencing. The young man soon joined her and offered his cigarette case. He noticed how the golden sunlight seemed to strike glints of steel blue from her dark hair. Her mouth was soft and generous and the slim column of her throat was as graceful as a swan's. She made a perfect picture.

'Thank you,' Kay said accepting one of his cigarettes. 'Do you feel like a tramp along the shore?'

'Why not. But mind how you get through the fence. I'll climb over first and help you.'

There was no need to do this, as Kay negotiated the fence quite easily. At the same time she wondered why an opening of some kind had not been provided. When they had gone a few yards she saw why there was no such entrance. A sign warned of the dangers of bathing at this particular point.

'What a shame!' Manson said. 'I'd love a swim about now. Oh, don't look so alarmed, Miss Ballard. At this time of year I'm never without trunks and towel.'

'You like swimming, Bruce? I enjoy it myself. There is a pool in Lynhaven, isn't there?'

There was, the young man told her. It was one that had been built within recent years. Summer and winter, Bruce went to the pool. For two years running he'd been a member of the local swimming team. Kay regarded him with fresh interest.

'Then you can hardly be described as a novice.'

'I've got two medals to prove that I'm

not. I am getting a trifle past it, though.'

'Rubbish!'

'I mean it,' he grinned. 'You don't remain in the top-flight for long. You go in young and you emerge when you're young. It doesn't prevent you joining in the fun, of course. The Neptune Club, we all enjoy ourselves. I'll drag you along one evening and introduce you to a crowd. You might find a friend or two. Ever met Simon's agent? Well, he used to be his agent. These days Simon is more in need of a kick in the pants than an agent.'

'Bruce!' Kay ejaculated. 'What a horrible thing to say! And about your own cousin . . . '

'Nevertheless it's true,' Manson said stubborny. 'Why can't he withdraw himself from his slough of despair? It isn't healthy. It isn't fair to his close associates. Caroline is dead and gone, and that is that.'

'You were speaking of Mr Lambert — Simon's agent,' Kay reminded him, her speculations beginning to run riot.

'Oh, yes, the club. I was just going to mention that Hal is a member. Marvellous swimmer. Simon used to be our star however.'

'Mr Nash?'

Manson grinned wryly. 'Why not? He was a grand swimmer, diver too. He still is, as a matter of fact. If only he would crawl out of his miserable shell.'

They had reached a headland where the sea breeze was unusually fresh and Kay brushed her hair from her forehead to watch three yachts scudding into the general direction of Lynhaven. Manson halted beside her, resting his hand lightly on her shoulder.

'There's a first-rate yachting club in town too,' he explained. 'I was a member for a while, but then I grew tired of it, sold my yacht to a chap for a song, and packed up.'

'So much for Sailor Manson! It requires a lot of skill and experience to handle them. I think I'd prefer a nice, luurious cabin-cruiser.'

'Simon had a fine one,' Manson said

musingly. 'If he's so sickened of the sea, why doesn't he sell Ashleigh and move inland?'

'Yes, it's odd why he hangs on after what happened to his wife. By the way, Bruce, his sister called yesterday, a few minutes before Mr Lambert arrived.'

'Then you've met both of them? What did you think of Cousin Lorna? Bit of a rum bird, isn't she?'

Here was an opportunity to pass on what Lorna had said regarding Caroline Nash. At the same time she might learn what Bruce's own views were on the late Mrs Nash. But would Manson relish a discussion of any form on the fate that had befallen Caroline? And had she not told herself it would be much better if she put Lorna and her gossip behind her? In spite of this, Kay was curious to have the young man's reactions.

'I don't know if I'd call Lorna a rum bird, Bruce. But she did say something that I found most disturbing.'

'About Caroline, I bet,' Manson said

grimly. 'She's determined to carry on her vendetta even beyond the grave.'

Kay shuddered involuntarily seaching the face of the other. 'I'm sorry, Bruce. I shouldn't have mentioned it. It is none of my business in any case. Shall we walk on a little further?'

'If you wish. No, don't worry about mentioning what Lorna might have said, Kay. She hated Caroline. She was of the opinion that Simon should have divorced her years ago.'

'Oh! Then there was some truth in what she insisted on relating to me?'

'Caroline and other men? Yes, there was. Caroline was a gay, fun-loving type. In those days Simon was something of a gay dog himself. Well, he was popular with a certain set. He was making a name for himself, and naturally there was the usual crowd of admirers following him around. One thing I'll say for him, though, he never took any of those scatter-brained females seriously. Perhaps Caroline didn't accept this. Perhaps she wasn't to be blamed, when she was left alone for weeks on end while Simon attended shows all over the country. If she turned to other men for companionship, who can say she was wrong?'

'But — but the boating accident, Bruce. Lorna believes it wasn't really an accident at all . . . '

'I can guess what she told you,' Manson cut in. 'There was a man on the cabin-cruiser the day it caught fire and sank. It's what the rumours maintained. It's what the newspaper reporters hinted at. Oh, I could tell you a lot more than that, Kay! You see, I was pretty friendly with Caroline myself. Well, it was to be expected, wasn't it? We were all one big happy family. Lambert had his eye on Caroline as well. In fact, it was through Hal that Simon met his wife in the first place. I couldn't say for sure, but I've deduced that Hal was beaten in the marriage stakes by a short head. There was a spell afterwards when he and Simon couldn't look at each other. But finally, with Simon and Caroline wed, things settled down. Until Simon began writing those big hits, that was. Then more excitement, more rumours of juicy scandal. Simon travelling abroad as well as in this country. Caroline left behind at home.'

'But surely she could have accompanied him on his travels?'

'She did at the beginning. Then the time came when she was expecting Diane . . . '

'Of course. I see.'

'The boating tragedy threw everything into an uproar,' Manson continued. 'The chap who was supposed to have seen someone in the *Morning Glory* with Caroline a short time before it caught fire was responsible for that. The police went to work with a vengeance. They interviewed everybody connected with the family. Even I came in for a rather fierce grilling.'

'You? But — '

'Why not? It was a period when everyone connected with Caroline came under suspicion. I dare say Lorna was partly responsible for keeping the fire burning. It developed she had been writing letters to Simon when he was absent from home. Do I have to tell you what she was saying about his wife in those letters?'

'But that was a horrible thing to do!'

'Lorna didn't seem to think so. She was of the opinion that Caroline was making six different kinds of fool of her brother, and she didn't mind who knew it . . . Well, there you are, Kay, if you didn't have a complete picture of the situation before, I imagine you have it now.'

She certainly had, Kay told herself hollowly. What her companion had just told her added depth and significance to a lot of things. Now she had a clearer outline of the situation at Ashleigh and the background to the present state of affairs there.

Lorna Nash emerged as an interfering busybody, on mischief bent since the day Caroline had become the composer's wife. How Simon Nash must have changed, if all she had gleaned about him so far was true.

What did he himself think of the accident which had cost his wife her life? Had he given credence to the rumours which had been rampant? Had he accepted the tales passed on to him by his own sister at their face value, or had he relied on forming his own conclusions and making his own assessment?

All these thoughts raced through her brain as she strolled on the seashore with Manson. Other questions posed themselves to her in rapid succession, but these were questions which she tried desperately to keep at bay. There were too terrible to dwell upon, even for the briefest of moments.

They arrived at a cluster of large rocks forming a raised vantage point where they could watch the sea and at the same time regard the country sweeping back from the road they had travelled. At Bruce's suggestion they took a seat and once more the young man produced his cigarette case.

'You've gone very silent of a sudden,' he remarked with a wry grin. 'Thinking over everything I've just said?'

She mustered a faint smile in response to this.

'It's difficult not to think about it, isn't it?'

'Why should you worry one way or another?' he argued equably. 'You'll be here for a matter of weeks and then be gone.'

'Yes, I know.'

His hand came over to fasten loosely on her fingers.

'Let's forget the drama at Ashleigh for a while, shall we? If the police failed to find a guilty person, you can be reasonably certain there wasn't one.'

'You don't believe there was, Bruce?'

He shrugged, a frown of annoyance flitting across his handsome features. The pressure of his hand on her fingers increased.

'Let's just say I'm not sure. Who can

be sure? The fuss and the turmoil have long since died down. Nowadays the tragedy is remembered by only a few.'

'Poor Simon,' Kay murmured. 'It must have been shattering for him.'

'Yes, it was. And what's more, it's time he was pulling himself up by the bootstraps and facing life afresh.'

Kay had an impulse just then to relate the conversation she had had with the composer, to tell Bruce that he felt, with the right influence brought to bear, he may be brought back to his musical career. Something held her back however; she wasn't sure what. Perhaps she didn't wish to divulge the peculiar footing she was approaching with Simon.

Simon, she thought breathlessly. Why was she thinking of him as Simon? Why did she wish it was he who was sitting here beside her instead of his cousin? Surely she couldn't be forming an attachment for the man! No, of course she wasn't. Such a thing was too ridiculous for words. As Bruce had pointed out, she would be here only for a matter of weeks and then be gone, back to Westcroft and Moorfield primary school. She would step straight out of the composer's life and never enter it again.

'Why the sad, forlorn expression, pray?'

'Don't tell me you can read my thoughts,' she cried with a forced laugh. 'Look, Bruce, I think I've had enough of the sea breezes for one evening. It's turning decidedly cool as well.'

'I really hadn't noticed it. I think it's quite warm. All right, I'll tell you what we'll do. There's a super little inn a few miles on along the coast from here. What do you say to going there and having a drink, something to eat too if you're peckish?'

Kay agreed at once. Anything was preferable to remaining for any longer at the seashore. Try as she did she couldn't rid her mind of a vision of Caroline Nash. She could clearly visualize the cabin-cruiser going up in flames, the panic that Caroline must have felt. And supposing — just supposing — there had been a man with her, a man who wished to get rid of her for some reason best known to himself, who had swum away when the boat had begun to sink and deliberately left her to her doom.

Bruce held on to her hand on the return walk over the beach path. Then, without warning, when they had a dozen yards to go to reach the fence, he drew her to him suddenly and implanted his lips on her own.

Kay broke away from him swiftly, her fingers going up to her mouth. Manson laughed gruffly, disappointment rendering his features repulsive. Odd how they seemed so to her at that moment.

'Good lord! I wasn't going to eat you. And what's a little kiss between friends?'

'That's strictly a matter of opinion, Bruce. If you wish to retain our friendly footing, you'd better restrain your enthusiasm, my lad.'

'Point taken, my fair lady. I consider myself thoroughly rebuffed. Shall we put it behind us with the rest and make a fresh start?'

Kay felt uneasy until she was seated beside him in his car once more. The remainder of the evening in his company was overshadowed by an air of tension which neither of them could ignore.

13

'You're back much earlier than I expected,' Simon Nash said when he met her in the hall. 'And why didn't Bruce stop off for a few minutes before running away? Surely nothing happened to frighten the poor fellow.'

The humour in the composer's voice and eyes was unmistakable, and despite her strained mood Kay joined in the brief chuckle he indulged in. Bruce Manson had driven up to the front door, but refused her invitation to come inside. No sooner had Kay alighted from his car than he accelerated away in a surge of speed.

'I did ask him to come in,' she answered. 'He turned me down. Perhaps he's in a hurry to keep another date.'

'So my cousin was disappointed in you. Miss Ballard. Well, I'm glad that someone has managed to trim him down to size.'

'Bruce fancies himself as a ladies' man?'

'Don't tell me you didn't gather as much?' the other rejoined, his dark eyes encompassing Kay in swift and keen appraisal. He had a cigarette between his fingers and puffed while Kay hesitated.

'Yes, I must admit that I did. He's harmless enough, though.'

'No doubt. So long as you endeavour to make him realize who is top dog.'

Kay excused herself and went on to the living-room. In a moment the composer followed her.

'Nicky and Diane went to bed at nine-thirty,' he explained. 'They wished to remain up until ten, but I wouldn't hear of it. I did the right thing, don't you think?'

'Yes, I do. Nine o'clock is late enough for them. I dare say Mrs Foley is in bed by now as well.'

'I believe so,' Simon Nash said. 'She

watched television for a while, but the programmes were poor this evening. A Western on both channels at the same time. You'd wonder they wouldn't get together and provide their public with a definite choice.'

Kay had the feeling he was engaging her in conversation for no other reason than to be talking with her. But if this was the case, why couldn't he come right out with it and suggest they sit down and chat for a while? The evening that Kay had put in with Bruce Manson, whilst providing her with some more shocks, had in no way tired her. Also, she usually found Simon Nash's company sufficiently stimulating to prove highly desirable.

'I suppose they imagine they must compete with each other at all levels,' she replied. 'Even at the expense of the viewers' irritation. Personally I enjoy Western films on television. I know that Nicholas shares my taste.'

'And how! I used to be very fond of them myself, but your tastes keep

changing, whether or not you like it
. . . Well — ' His tone became brisk.
' — I'd better leave you to your own
devices, Miss Ballard. You still find life
at Ashleigh bearable?'

'I'm continuing to enjoy it,' Kay said
with a smile. 'I'm growing quite
attached to the children.'

'Yes, I know. And they to you. It will
be a big wrench for them when you
pack your cases once more and set out
for your own home.'

This was a subject which Kay was
reluctant to dwell upon. It wouldn't be
such a wrench, she explained, not when
the children would be returning to their
respective boarding schools and renew-
ing the friendships they had forged
there.

The composer inclined his head. 'I'm
sure you're right. And children do
adapt quickly. It doesn't alter the fact
that Diane thinks the world of you,
Miss Ballard.'

'She's a dear girl, Mr Nash. She'll
grow into a splendid young woman. In

a few years you won't recognize her as the girl she is now.'

'Sad in a way, is it not?' he murmured wistfully.

'I would hesitate to agree. Why shouldn't she grow up and become a woman? It won't be long either until Nicholas is a man.'

'He's a grand chap, isn't he?' Here was a happier reaction.

'Adorable.' Kay began moving on to the kitchen. Surely the composer had said all he intended saying for tonight. Still he lingered, reluctant to leave her, it seemed. Perhaps he hoped she would offer to make him a cup of tea or coffee. No sooner had the thought crossed Kay's mind than she uttered it.

'Oh, yes. I'd love a cup of coffee, if it's not too much trouble. Didn't Cousin Bruce treat you to a meal before bringing you home?' he added with a glint in his eye.

'Yes, he did. But it seems ages ago.'

'Why not have a snack then?'

'Golly, I'd be certain to have

indigestion if I ate anything at this time of night! Are you hungry yourself?'

'I am a trifle peckish,' the other admitted, his grin ingenuous.

'In that case I'll risk Mrs Foley's wrath and prepare a few sandwiches. Where shall we eat — right here in the kitchen?'

'Why not?'

Kay made the coffee and sandwiches while the composer perched on a stool and looked on. Kay was aware of yet another gradual change in their relationship as Simon Nash chatted on all sorts of subjects, asking what she thought about this, what her reaction would be to that. Kay responded quite frankly and unselfconsciously. There was an atmosphere of intimacy between them just then, and before their snack was finished they had broken the barrier of formality which indicated that Kay should be Miss Ballard and the composer should be Mr Nash.

'Why can't we address each other by our first names?' he reasoned. 'There is no merit or virtue in stiffness that I can find.'

'I agree with you entirely. But I'm sure the children will have a pink fit if they hear us calling each other Kay and Simon.'

'We can be stiff when they're around if you'd rather we should preserve our dignity in their eyes.'

Kay laughed merrily. Here was a hint of the old Simon Nash coming to the fore. She wished she had known him before the tragedy which had changed his personality and outlook. Yet, there was hope of her witnessing a second transformation, and this one for the better. What vain ambitions she harboured!

'Perhaps we should. Now ... I'd better wash up these things and stow them away before Mrs Foley sees anything amiss.'

'I'll leave you to it,' the composer said. 'For me the night is still young enough. Do you know, Kay, I may go up to my music room and have another bash at the old piano.'

Kay's eyes sparkled. For an instant she experienced an unaccountable tugging in her breast. Here was a startling change of face.

'Bash is the word,' she smiled. 'Go up there and throw all your inhibitions to the winds. If the muse won't come to you, then you must, at least, announce that you're still around and very much in business.'

'You really mean that, don't you? Oh, Miss Ballard, I'd give anything to be able to sit down at the piano and compose a tune! Just one little tune would give me the necessary encouragement to persevere.'

'Please do it then,' the girl urged excitedly.

They were behaving like two kids, Kay reflected fleetingly — a boy and girl who, having kept their distance for reasons best known to themselves, had decided to shun their shells and make an effort to get to know each other better.

'You promised you would help me,' her companion reminded her.

'How?' Kay demanded from a tightening throat. 'Provide you with the requisite inspiration? I'm afraid I haven't had a lot of practice doing that. No one has ever found me particularly inspiring.'

'No one has ever exploited the possibilities, you should say. But . . . I'll be keeping you out of your bed. And it is after ten. If Mrs Foley hears us, she'll assume we're both crazy.'

'Once Mrs Foley falls asleep, she sleeps soundly,' Kay informed him. 'She told me so when — when — '

'When you heard me at the piano and wondered what the devil sort of maniac I was?' he finished for her.

Kay laughed again, on this occasion with more restraint. Simon Nash was staring at her in an odd sort of way, and she found his gaze disturbingly hypnotic.

'I was alarmed until I learned the truth. Simon. Listen . . . I am not in the least tired. I am burning with enthusiasm. I am positively quaking.'

'Quaking?' he echoed wonderingly.

'Yes. There is no other word to describe the sensation adequately. Supposing that I — Kay Ballard, schoolteacher ordinary — proved to be the means of you regaining your touch as a composer?'

'Please, Kay! Less of the dramatics. You surely aren't so easily impressed.'

'That, my dear sir, is a luxury I should be entitled to. Shall we proceed to the haunts of the muses and conduct the experiment forthwith?'

They negotiated the staircase like a pair of conspirators. As they passed Mrs Foley's bedroom on their way to the door at the end of the passage, Kay had a distinct qualm. What on earth would the cook think if she could see her slinking in this fashion with Simon Nash?

Simon produced a key and inserted it in the lock, explaining in a whisper that the purpose of the lock was to prevent the children gaining entrance.

'It dates back to when they were much younger and more liable to go on the prowl. Nowadays they accept the locked room as part of the general enigma.'

'Diane never queries your neglect of your music?' Kay asked him when they were inside the room and the door had been closed firmly behind them.

'Yes, she does. She's no mean pianist herself. She used to practice my pieces until I detested the sound of them.'

The room was a small one, containing only the large piano, a small table and two easy chairs. There was one wall shelf where piles of manuscript were stored. When Kay turned to look at the composer she noticed a sheen of perspiration on his brow. It was as though even coming into this room had a peculiar effect on him. She repressed a sympathetic shudder.

'I'm rather fond of the piano myself,' she said boldly.

'Then you can play?'

'A little. What have we at hand?' As she spoke she lifted a sheet of music from the piano top. It was in a crumpled state, as if it had been grasped roughly and squeezed into a bundle. Kay took the stool at the keyboard and straightened out the sheet before her.

'I can't stand that, Kay,' Simon said then.

'What is it?' Kay murmured, ignoring the inflection in his voice. ' 'There was a heart'. I don't know why you can't stand it, Simon. It's one of my favourite melodies. Do you have objections to my playing it?'

'I might commence screaming,' he threatened, simulating a levity at odds with his expression.

He stood at her back while she ran over the opening bars. In another moment Kay was humming the tune. Finally, caught up by the sheer beauty of the music she began to sing softly.

'There was a heart that dwelt in
    lonely places

Until a day when you came into
   view . . . '

'Please stop it, Kay!'
Kay's voice tailed away and she
raised her eyes questioningly to those of
Simon Nash, seeing the pain that held
him just then, the agony of spirit he was
so obviously suffering.
'I'm sorry, Simon. I do realize I
haven't the sweetest voice in the world,
but — '
'Drat it, Miss Ballard,' he snapped. 'It
has got nothing to do with your voice.
Indeed if you must know, you have a
good voice.'
'Then why can't I sing your song? If
you can't bear this particular one
— and goodness knows why — then I
shall choose a different one.'
'No, you shall not.'
It was utterly hopeless, Kay realized.
She had made a supreme effort to
unlock whatever door he had closed
against himself, without even a modi-
cum of success. She sighed and rose

from the piano stool. Simon Nash was puffing furiously at the cigarette he had lighted. He was in a state of extreme agitation, she saw. Had it to do solely with this particular song she had chosen, or did all of his compositions revive hurtful memories of the past?

That was the root of the matter, she was certain. Most of what he had written had been inspired by his wife. Whenever he heard his music — whenever he even contemplated it — the painful memories insisted on resurrecting themselves, to hurt and punish him.

Punish? No, surely that wasn't so. Why was she thinking in this vein? Because of what she had learned from Bruce Manson this evening? Was Simon Nash the victim of a sense of guilt?

Desperately Kay endeavoured to brush these thoughts from her mind. She accepted a cigarette from the case he extended, permitted him to hold his lighter for her. A strained silence came between them.

'What are you afraid of, Simon?'

'Afraid! Good heavens, girl, you do come out with the odd remarks, don't you.'

'But you must be afraid,' Kay insisted steadily. 'I could read it in your face immediately we came in here. The whole atmosphere changed at once. Oh, don't imagine that I wish to pry into any of your business or your personal affairs. It would be the last thing I would dream of doing. But you said you would make an effort. If you don't start somewhere, you will never get anywhere.'

'That is a charming gem of observation and no mistake. Charming if not exactly original.'

'There is no need to mock me,' Kay said with a trace of asperity in her tone.

'My dear Kay, I am not mocking you. It — it's just — Oh, hang it all, I don't know how to commence to explain.'

'There is no need to explain, Simon. Perhaps I can guess why you have neglected your work for so long, why you can't bring yourself to consider it, even. I don't blame you. Who could blame you? But if you'd only realize how you're depriving the world of your music, your talent — '

'Rubbish!' the other cut in harshly.

'It is not rubbish. It is the truth. It — ' Here Kay stopped talking and brought her lips together firmly. There was an ashtray on the piano top where she deposited her partly-smoked ciga-rette. Her companion didn't speak until she had turned to gain the door.

'Where are you going, Kay?'

'To bed. It's getting late, and if I'm to be in the best of moods for the children in the morning, it's time I was turning in.'

'Very well. I might stay here for a few minutes. Thank you for trying to help the struggling artist,' he added with a weak grin. 'It looks as if I'm beyond assistance or encouragement.'

'If you tell yourself so, then you undoubtedly are,' Kay returned and went on out of the room.

In the seclusion of her own bedroom,

she sat at her dressing table and gave rein to the reflections which persisted in passing through her mind.

Was it possible, she wondered, that there had been a man in the cabin cruiser on the day it caught fire and sank? Was it possible also that Caroline Nash's companion on the boat had been none other than her husband?

'Oh, no, no!' she whispered in horror. 'Simon couldn't have wished such a thing on his wife. He couldn't be a murderer.'

Still, if Caroline Nash had been deliberately murdered, someone had to be guilty of the awful act. Who? Surely not Hal Lambert who, if Bruce Manson was to be believed, had been as deeply in love with the woman as Simon? Surely not Bruce Manson himself, who had admitted his admiration for the composer's wife?

Adding these possibilities to the tale which Lorna Nash had told her, the result was positively alarming. It could mean that Caroline did have a lover who had grown tired of her and who wished to throw her over, and then, when she threatened to divulge the association to her husband as a blackmail attempt, this same lover had planned to do away with her in a manner that would appear accidental.

Yet, if so much rumour persisted, it was bound to have reached the ears of the police. Why then hadn't the police seen fit to apprehend someone on suspicion of being the murderer? This was a silly deduction, she realized. Even the police would not dare to arrest a person without the necessary evidence and opportunity to prove their case.

In bed at last, Kay strove to clear her mind of the numerous speculations and doubts which plagued her. She had not heard Simon Nash leave his studio and wondered if he was still in there, still wrestling with himself, with the inhibitions that had a strangle-hold on him, with his conscience perhaps.

A long time later she was dropping off to sleep when the sound of the piano being played insinuated itself on her conscienceness. At first Kay believed herself to be enmeshed in a dream-like state and that the music had no existence outside her fancy. But then, when she realized that she was actually awake and that, moreover, the composer really was fingering the keyboard of his piano, she jerked upright in bed and concentrated on listening

Simon's playing was muted, gentle, as though he were caressing the notes other than striking them, as though that, having coaxed music to emerge from the instrument, he was reluctant to assert himself and the mastery he was capable of.

The playing stopped and Kay held her breath during the interval before it was resumed. He had played a few bars, tentatively and exploratory, and now he was repeating the snatch of melody. Yes, it was a melody and, what was more, an entirely new one in Kay's experience.

'He has commenced composing again!'

Not pausing to think, Kay dashed from her bed and drew her dressing gown about her. Then she left her room and approached the door at the end of the passage. She paused there, nervous and undecided. The piano was tinkling again. The bars were repeated and, immediately, another was added to them.

Kay pressed against the door and it opened under her pressure. She stepped into the studio and the composer spun on his stool, eyes shining with a confidence she had never seen in him.

'You've done it!' he whispered hoarsely. 'Your magic wand has done the trick, Kay. I'm back on the treadmill again!'

14

There seemed to be a different air about the big house next morning. It was as if everything was hushed and waiting, hopeful, and at the same time, slightly apprehensive. Simon Nash was absent when Kay and the children sat down at the table to eat breakfast, and immediately Diane asked Nancy where her father was.

'Your father is still asleep,' the maid returned in an awed voice. 'Haven't you two heard the latest?'

'We've guessed there is something unusual going on,' the girl rejoined with a little frown directed at Kay. 'But what?'

'Mrs Foley heard him,' the maid whispered. She was behaving like a person who had been sworn to secrecy, but who would die, or at the very least suffocate, if she didn't have the chance to tell what she knew.

'Mrs Foley heard whom?' Diane demanded in some concern. Nancy, are you referring to Daddy by any chance?'

'Of course I am. Who did you think I was referring to? Did you hear him as well, Miss Ballard?'

'Yes,' Kay nodded, stifling a smile and evading the sharp glance that Diane stabbed at her. She had remained with Simon Nash for a bare thirty minutes last night, but it had been long enough for her to be certain that he really had recovered his enthusiasm and his old touch. When Kay left him he was still in the throes of creative work.

'I might have a new song finished by morning,' he had informed her happily.

'Morning!' Kay had echoed. 'But you're surely not going to stay at your piano until morning?'

At which Simon Nash had laughed merrily and clutched Kay's fingers. 'My dear Kay, all my best work was done in the wee small hours, so you don't have to distress yourself. But what you must do is congratulate yourself. Whether or not you want to believe it, Kay, you have applied the spark I was waiting for, the inspiration that I needed. I am composing this melody because of you and therefore for you.'

Kay had waited to hear no more. Had she done so she would have burst into tears. She was sure she would have done this, and made the most awful baby out of herself. But even when she slipped into bed again, she could not sleep, but lay, thinking her fevered thoughts and at the same time straining her ears to listen to the composition which Simon was struggling with.

'Then what was Daddy doing that is so amusing to Nancy, Miss Ballard?' Diane continued. 'He surely wasn't drunk and dancing a jig on the roof.'

'Such a thing to say about your own father!' Nancy cried. 'Now if I were your parent, my girl — '

'Oh, Nancy, do be reasonable.' Diane interrupted her. 'And please unravel this mystery before I die of suspense.'

'Your father was at his piano last night,' Nancy said.

'Playing?' the girl asked in a new tone. 'As he used to play long ago?'

'That's right, Diane,' Kay supplied. 'Isn't it wonderful? Last night he began to write a new song. Perhaps it will turn out to be only part of a musical. But once started, he'll keep on working now.'

'I hope you've proved correct, Miss Ballard. Daddy was only happy when he was composing something or other.'

That morning Kay took the children to the nearby woods. It as another splendid July morning, with clear skies and a brilliant sun, and the excursion to the woods was conducted at the request of Nicholas. It was after eleven when they returned to Ashleigh, but even at that time there was no sign of Simon Nash.

'I took his breakfast up to him,' Nancy explained. 'He said he might go straight to his studio without coming down.'

'But he shouldn't do that,' Kay said. 'He should have a walk in the air before he shuts himself up again.'

'Then you'd better tell him, Miss Ballard,' the maid smiled. 'He might pay more heed to you than he would to me.'

Much later Kay did hear the piano being played in the room at the end of the passage. She was in her own room at the time, and was tempted to go along to Simon and advise him to take a break in the fresh air. She resisted the idea however, deciding that it might be unwise to interfere until he finished what he was working at. After all, it would be a pity if he suddenly lost his will to compose just as easily as he had recovered it.

Kay was downstairs again when the telephone rang, and, as she was the nearest to it just then, she went to the instrument to speak to the caller. The caller was Bruce Manson, who greeted Kay rather sheepishly.

'I didn't make much of a hit with

you, Kay,' he said with a feeble laugh. 'But maybe it was because I applied the wrong technique in your case.'

'Is that so? I suppose you have a whole range of techniques which you like to experiment with.'

Manson answered with another laugh. 'I asked for it, didn't I? What I'm getting at is this: could we wipe the slate clean like a good little school-teacher, and commence on an entirely new story?

'With a brand new technique, of course!'

'Please, Kay! Don't be too hard on me. I am a comparative novice after all.'

'Yes,' Kay said grimly. 'You demonstrated that to the satisfaction of no one but yourself. Oh, listen, Bruce, I must tell you about Simon . . . '

'Must you?' Manson wondered with little interest. 'Has he gone and grown two heads or something? I've been waiting for old Simon to come up with something spectacular. He hasn't fallen off one of those cliffs and dented his vanity?'

'You really love him, Bruce.'

'Oh, I can take him or leave him,' Manson chuckled. 'Seriously, Kay, what has he been up to?'

'Composing,' Kay said.

'No! I don't believe it.'

'Yes,' Kay chuckled. 'It's true. By this time he may have a new song finished'

Manson's voice changed from a mildly bantering to a brisk and serious note.

'You really are saying that Simon is back at his music, Kay? I mean, you couldn't be mistaken, could you? He must have made a million abortive attempts to woo back his genius, but always the results were negative.'

'Not this time. Why don't you come and see him if you find it hard to swallow?'

'Yes, I might,' Manson replid slowly. 'Well, what do you know! We've got a miracle on our hands . . . But, Kay, what happens if the thing he's working on is no good?'

'I don't understand you,' the girl frowned. 'How can it be no good? I heard part of the melody and it's heavenly.'

'Imagine that now!'

'There is no need to be sarcastic, Bruce.'

'I'm not being sarcastic, teacher, I'm giving vent to a genuine wave of wonder. Well, my lass, if what you say is true, prepare yourself for the patter of a variety of sizes of feet.'

'I — I don't understand, Bruce . . . '

'Don't worry, Kay, you will. Look, I'm signing off now, but I promise to see you soon.'

'I can't wait.'

'I just bet you can't! You're an expert at handing out the perfect brush-off, Miss Ballard. Oh, it has only occurred to me. Have you told Hal? Has anyone told Hal?'

'Hal — You're talking about Mr Lambert? Simon's agent?'

'Ah! So Mr Nash has become Simon? Well, well now! And he has suddenly found his old punch. Put all that together and what do you get? Don't bother to anwer, Kay. I think I know what I get.'

'I fail to understand a word of what you're saying,' Kay choked, her cheeks blazing.

'As I've already advised you, teacher, don't worry. It might never happen. If it does I'll make that darned composer eat his own piano. Legs and all!'

'Oh!' Kay exploded when the young man had hung up. 'Of all the confounded nerve. And who does he imagine he's talking to and about anyhow?'

'Is something the matter, Miss Ballard?'

Kay swung to find the maid staring keenly at her. The colour already staining her skin deepened.

'Nothing is the matter, Nancy,' she responded thickly. 'What gave you the notion that there was?'

'I fancied you were talking to yourself just then.'

'Really, Nancy! Of course I wasn't talking to myself. Has — has Mr Nash come down from his room yet?'

'I haven't seen him,' Nancy confessed. She came closer to Kay and her eyes sparkled with excitement. 'You've no idea what it will be like here if the public learns that Mr Nash is composing again,' she added in a tense whisper.

Suddenly Kay was aware of cold fingers tracing her spine.

'Are — are you saying there used to be — '

'It was practically an open house,' Nancy gushed on. 'People coming in at all times of the day. All sorts of people. Musicians, orchestra leaders. And the women . . . '

'What women?' Kay gasped.

'Admirers of Mr Nash. Especially Nina Fellowes. That gorgeous redhead who recorded a lot of Mr Nash's songs.'

'Oh, no!' Kay groaned.

'Don't upset yourself, Miss Ballard. It might not happen at all. Not if we all keep it a secret.'

'A secret! Good heavens, Nancy, what have I done? I was speaking with Bruce Manson just then. I — I told him that Mr Nash was busily composing. Supposing he decides to tell somebody? And he did mention Hal Lambert!'

'You could ring him back.' Nancy suggested. 'It's none of my business, of course, but Mr Nash might not want to create a fuss.'

'You're right, Nancy. Quickly! What is Bruce's number? I haven't bothered to check his telephone number.'

The maid had no idea what Bruce's telephone number was, but she believed it was marked in the directory which was at hand. Kay immediately fingered through the pages, and sure enough, Manson's name was marked with a small circle. She dialled swiftly, but failed to get response.

'He was gone out,' she panted finally. 'Now the fat is in the fire with a vengeance. What can I do, Nancy?'

'Nothing much,' the girl replied. 'The only thing you can do is keep your fingers crossed and hope Mr Manson holds his tongue.'

Kay was in the library a short time later when the telephone rang shrilly. Bruce, she thought and hurried to take the call before someone else did. This time she found herself speaking with Hal Lambert.

'Hello, Miss Ballard,' the agent said. 'Is the big chief in evidence at the moment?'

'He is busy, Mr Lambert. I mean, he is in his room.'

'His office off the library? Then you can put me through to him?'

'No, not his office! Upstairs. Look, Mr Lambert, perhaps I could take a message for him?'

'Oh, no, you can't, Miss Ballard! Bruce was in touch a short time ago. He says that Simon is back to porridge. Have you any evidence to support that statement?'

'I'm afraid I can't say, Mr Lambert,' Kay replied desperately, realizing she had started something that could very well snowball into monstrous proportion.

'Odd!' Lambert grunted. 'Never mind. I'll get into my car and drive over there straightaway.'

Hanging up, Kay wondered if she should seek out Simon and confess what she had said to Bruce Manson. But no, she wouldn't. There was no telling how the composer might react. Better that events run their natural course. Natural course! There was a laugh. Had she minded her own business and followed Simon Nash to look after his own, there would be no need for her to worry at all.

Hal Lambert was as good as his word. In less than twenty minutes later he drove up to the front door of Ashleigh and strode in without bothering to announce himself. Kay, who had been waiting in readiness for his visit, waylaid the agent in the hall.

'Ah, there you are, Miss Ballard. Has Simon emerged yet, do you know?'

Kay shook her head. 'It was I who

told Bruce Manson,' she explained anxiously. 'Perhaps I made a mistake.'

'As a matter of fact, Bruce did divulge that,' Lambert grinned. 'But don't distress yourself. I'm the very soul of discretion when I have to be. And now, if you don't mind, I'll go on up to the studio and see how he's making out.'

It was only the beginning of the avalanche, as Kay was to find out soon. There was a veritable stream of telephone calls throughout the day. It showed Kay how, when he'd ceased to be active as a composer, Simon's friends and acquaintances had gradually but surely withdrawn from his circle, and how that circle of friends and acquaintances had diminished until very few were left, and those only his relations and closest friends.

Now that the news had leaked out — via Kay initially to Simon's cousin. Bruce — and then quickly been spread — it appeared that the interest in the composer and his popularity were in fresh spate.

All through the lunch hour Kay was occupied in answering the doorbell when she wasn't dealing with the telephone. Nancy and she formed a sort of relay team, dividing the duties between them. Hal Lambert and a couple of other people whom Kay had never seen, much less knew remained for lunch, so that there was extra work for Mrs Foley and which Kay felt obliged to share in also.

'You'd think we'd been visited by royalty,' Nancy remarked at one stage. 'And I did warn you, Miss Ballard.'

'Indeed you did. But it came much too late, Nancy. The damage was done before I could even think about it.'

The drawing-room was taken over exclusively for the composer and his agent, and people from the recording companies with whom he was supposed to be under contact. During this hectic period Kay saw Simon only once or twice. He had really changed now, she noticed. Gone was his air of brooding and detachment, the cloak of cool indifference he had drawn about him and held on to for almost three years. A new light shone in his eye; fresh confidence and enthusiasm seemed to surround him like a halo. At least he bore her no ill-will, Kay consoled herself. In fact if his demeanour was anything to judge by, he was in his element.

During all the furore, Diane and Nicholas contented themselves to remaining on the fringe of events, yet it was patent that Diane at least was enjoying the whole thing enormously.

'That is what it used to be like when I was younger,' she told Kay at one stage when Kay was snatching a cup of coffee in the kitchen with Nancy and Mrs Foley. 'But you must remember it, Mrs Foley.'

'Indeed I do, child. I remember too being worn out every night. But I did have a rare old time all the same. There was plenty of life and fun and laughter.'

'And Mummy,' the girl raced on, 'she took charge of everything. Absolutely took charge. But then my Daddy would go away . . .'

For Kay it cast a cloud over the proceedings. But not for long. There was so much to do there was scarcely time to think. She met Lorna Nash again, and in the early evening Nina Fellowes arrived. The redhead's beauty took her breath away.

Inevitably, the evening finished up with a party. George Mallows had been sent off to Lynhaven post-haste for extra foodstuffs and champagne and all manner of drinks. The party was held in the drawing-room, which was the biggest room the house boasted. There were a score of people present, Kay calculated, some of whom were known and introduced to her, and others whom she guessed were newspaper representatives.

One of these gentlemen drew Kay aside and smilingly introduced himself as Horace Travers.

'The Lynhaven Beacon, you know, Miss Ballard. You're a school-teacher, aren't you? All the way from Westcroft? I believe you came here in the capacity of companion to Mr Nash's children?'

'That's true,' Kay agreed to the rapid questions he fired at her. 'But surely that doesn't make news in this day and age?'

'Ah, you can't fool me,' the reporter grinned. 'We've all heard the story.'

'What story, for heaven's sake!' Kay gulped.

'Come, come, Miss Ballard. Modesty is all very well in its place, but this is hardly the time nor place for it. It was through meeting you that Mr Nash was inspired to compose this new piece that he's done.'

'You're crazy!'

'That's good, Miss Ballard. Hold it for a second. Right, Roy, come and get it!'

Next second a flash-bulb blinded Kay. She tried to get beyond the range of the camera-man. Relentlessly he followed up, as became any zealous exponent of his calling.

'Just one more, Miss Ballard!'

'Oh, please stop this nonsense and leave me alone.'

Seeing her chance, Kay sprang for the door, burst through and beat a hasty retreat to the sanctuary of the kitchen and the comforting presence of Mrs Foley.

'Why, Kay, lass, what it the matter with you? They're tossing too much champagne around, I'll warrant.'

'It's those awful newspaper men, Mrs Foley. They refuse to leave me alone. They're saying I inspired Mr Nash to commence composing again. They took my photograph. It will all be in the newspapers.'

'And why not?' the homely woman laughed.

'Why not!' Kay echoed, and then, on the next moment, burst into tears.

How could Simon Nash do such a thing to her . . .

15

It was a long time later when Kay had the opportunity of seeing the composer on his own. Indeed, the time was after midnight, and Kay had just closed the door of her bedroom behind her when it was rapped again on the very next instant.

She opened the door to Simon Nash.

'Forgive me, Kay,' he began. 'I didn't have a minute all day to say a word to you.'

'No,' Kay responded with a weak smile. 'You were kept far too busy, weren't you? Everyone was kept too busy to take time off to breathe.'

'Are you going to bed directly?'

'Well, I — '

'It's a silly question. I bet you're ready for it. But I thought you might spare me just a few moments . . . '

Not in her bedroom, surely, Kay

thought. The composer's next words indicated what he had in mind.

'If we could go into the studio,' he suggested.

'Of course.'

In the studio Kay heaved a sigh and brushed a tendril of hair off her forhead. Simon Nash offered cigarettes but she shook her head.

'I've smoked far too much today, thank you,' she said with a short laugh. 'Drank too much too, I dare say. But no, I didn't really. That terrible newspaper man kept plying me with drinks he said were harmless fruit juices, but they were the most potent fruit juices I've ever experienced. I realized what he was trying to do and played him at his own game.'

'That is mainly why I wished to speak to you, Kay. Somehow or other — and it will be quite useless asking me why — they heard a whisper that you were responsible for my breaking my long musical silence.'

'Don't I know!' Kay groaned.

'Then you can guess at the type of story they'll plaster over the fronts of all the papers?'

'Yes, I certainly can, Simon.'

'Does it bother you so much?' he queried anxiously.

'Bother me? Well, I — Yes, naturally it bothers me. After all, these stupid people are going to draw conclusions that have no basis in fact. They'll tell their readers that a marvellous romance is brewing between the great composer, Simon Nash and his children's companion, school-teacher, Kay Ballard. Oh, you know as well as I what they will say, Simon.'

'I do,' he replied slowly. A slight frown had puckered his brow and he took a puff from the cigarette he held. 'It is somewhat unfortunate, I suppose. The point is, Kay, will it bother you *that* much?'

Kay's own brow gathered now as she stared at him.

'I don't think so. Apart from the irritation of having your name coupled with a man who . . .' Here Kay's voice tailed away and her cheeks darkened.

'That's it!' Simon Nash sighed and nodded heavily. 'I'm sure the last thing you desire is to have your name linked with mine — even though I do happen to have a reputation of sorts.'

Kay's throat was suddenly dry.

'I — I — Simon, I'm afraid you're approaching this from the wrong angle,' she stammered at length. 'Having your name coupled with my own in the newspapers will not cause me any embarassment. It's you I am thinking of.'

'What! But I thought — '

'What did you think?' Kay urged when he in turn broke off. 'Now please don't get the impression at the other extreme. Many a girl would give her arm to be remarked on as the person who had revived your inspiration and your will to work. Personally, I do feel it a great honour. But it's an honour I'd be reluctant to accept with a clear conscience.'

The composer gave a gruff laugh.

'What *are* you talking about, Kay?' he demanded. 'You get more ambiguous by the minute. First you say you are happy to be associated with something, and then you say you are not. Surely it must be one thing or the other.'

'Let me explain, Simon. All this talk of receiving inspiration, or anything else from me or from anyone else, has been blown up out of all proportion to the fundamental facts.'

'Indeed!' Nash murmured ominously. 'But that isn't a very full or satisfying explanation, my dear Miss Ballard.'

'Oh, let's look at everything in its proper perspective,' Kay argued patiently. 'You went off composing for a long time. No doubt there were definite physical factors which have to bear a certain amount of responsibility, but those don't comprise the entire story.'

'You get more intriguing now! Please continue.'

Kay did. She was not solely responsible for the stroke of good fortune which had befallen him, she stressed Even if she had never come to Ashleigh, Simon Nash would still have recovered his ability and enthusiasm to work.

'The greatest nonsense I have heard in a life-time!' he erupted.

'It isn't nonsense, Simon. If you weren't so taken up with heaping laurels over me, you would reason it out for yourself.'

'You don't wish to be a partner in my success?' he said sharply.

'You're twisting my words, Simon. And another thing,' Kay ran on swiftly, 'what about this new piece you are supposed to have written? Through all the fuss and fun and flying champagne corks, I never heard a person evince the slightest curiosity over what you had or had not composed. It seemed to me that any excuse was sufficient to initiate a party, which makes a lot of people little better than hypocrites, in my estimation.'

'There is a certain truth in that, I won't doubt,' he replied. 'But here — You aren't attempting to make out that I am daft enough to masquerade under false pretences?'

'Indeed, no!' Kay said hastily. 'I can say at the very least that I was in on the birth of your new melody. I can say too that I was the first person other than yourself to hear it being created.'

'Fine,' he said with an uneasy grin. 'Then we do know that *something* exists?'

'Oh, heavens! I keep saying the wrong things. You must take me for an awful pessimist, Simon.'

'On the contrary, I take you for the complete optimist. It is a fallacy to suppose that the optimist must, of necessity, be silly and irrational. To my mind, an optimist is a person who, whilst recognizing the weak points of a situation, remains hopeful of its resolving itself eventually. And now, Kay, if you've got a couple more minutes to spare in which to bear with me, I shall endeavour to prove beyond fear of contradiction that I have written a new melody. Let's call it a song for the present. There might be others which can be strung together. Hal is under the delusion that at last we've got the foundations for a full-length musical.'

'That would be wonderful! Yes, I would love to hear the piece which you composed. I might tell you that I have already memorized the opening bars.'

'Then they must have something! Take a seat and lend an ear, my fair one.'

They both laughed and seated themselves, Kay on one of the easy chairs close to the piano, and Simon Nash on the piano stool. The sheet of manuscript he had completed he handled with a gentleness approaching reverence, unfolding it and placing it before him. The strong, musician's fingers hovered above the keys.

'Are we ready?'

'Yes,' Kay whispered, rejecting the levity he chose to inject into his tone. It was spurious, she knew, a shield to cover up the true feelings which possessed him. Yet she did not hold this against him in any way.

For a space Kay sat entranced as those fingers wove a pattern of exquisite beauty. The piece was exactly in the mould that had produced all that other music from Simon Nash. There was no doubt of any kind that he had acquired his old touch. But that wasn't the entire picture. A new element had been introduced, consciously or unconsciously, which served to enhance the overall result. There was a sense of hopefulness in this music, but a poignancy too, subtly blended in a way that soon had Kay's eyes stinging.

Finally his fingers were still. For a fleeting second Simon Nash sat there, head raised, eyes focused on some far-off object. Some goal he had been straining to achieve? Or some intangible breath of nostalgia that he trusted he had succeeded, if only to some degree, in recapturing?

Kay did not know. She did know that she had gone through some traumatic experience. She suspected this had been shared by the man who sat at the piano. He turned his head to her, a faint smile grooving his mouth, his gaze expectant.

'Well, Kay, what did you think of it?'

'It — it was splendid, Simon. It is the most suitable word I can think of. Is there anything which can surpass splendour?'

He shrugged, boyishly shy now. 'I really don't know. And now, would you like to read the lyric? I shan't endeavour to sing it, as I've never deluded myself regarding the croak that persists in emerging as my singing voice. It's in the rough at the moment, of course — the lyric, naturally! — and will require a little polishing. But you can catch the general gist.'

He extended the manuscript and Kay took it from him. The title of the piece leaped from the paper at her. '*Because Of You.*' She stared at it in silence for an instant, then glanced at him.

'You — you have dedicated it to your late wife?'

'Read it, Kay,' he urged roughly.

Kay did, her heart lurching as the words and their meaning revealed themselves to her. By the time she had finished reading her eyes were misted in tears.

'Oh, no, Simon, you can't!' It was obvious whom the lyric and the music were intended for. But no, he couldn't do this. He simply couldn't . . .

'Why can't I?'

'Because, because — Simon, I didn't do all that much for you. I did only what any sensible and sympathetic person could have done in the same circumstances.'

'You're wrong, you know,' he said quietly and with a timbre in his tone that sent another shock running riot in Kay. 'You'd be totally dishonest if you didn't admit it.'

He vacated his stool then, pushing it aside. Now he was standing in front of her, towering over her. Looking into his dark eyes, Kay was aware of a sudden panic welling in her being.

'No,' she panted. 'No!'

She flung the sheet of music from her and wheeled to gain the door. She didn't reach it however. Simon's hand stretched out and his fingers caught her arm, the pressure gentle enough, but firm enough for all that.

Breast heaving, Kay turned to face him. Then, as though the madness of the moment was determined to run its course, he drew her into his arms. His features were looming above her own. His gaze was encompassing her. His mouth was descending to hers.

Kay had no power to move, no power to reject this madness that insisted on overwhelming them. Their lips met in a tentative contact of wonderment. The kiss that followed wiped all else from Kay's consciousness.

She was barely aware that he had released her and stepped back from her. Now she saw pain in his eyes — the pain of what — disappointment? Rejection? Disillusion?

Kay swayed and might have fallen had he not clutched her in his arms once more. She wanted to release herself, but was lacking in the necessary will to do so. She wanted to tear herself free and rush off to the safety and seclusion and haven of her own room, but was unable to initiate the motions.

'Should I say that I'm sorry, Kay?'

She didn't answer him, just continued to lean against him and pray that strength would return to her limbs, that courage would reassert itself and rescue her from the fate that yawned before her. What fate? What did she fear? She saw nothing in the eyes of Simon Nash but a vast tenderness, a great love.

'No, Simon, no . . .'

'You mean that I should be sorry?'

'I — I — Oh, I don't know what I mean. I don't know what this is I feel. I just imagine that you — '

'Have taken advantage of you? Believe me, if you think so, then I am sorry. More sorry than you can ever guess. I yielded to an impulse then. I did what any other man would have done in the circumstances.'

'What circumstances?' Kay gulped. 'Listen, Simon,' she rushed on swiftly. 'Don't allow whatever sense of gratitude you may feel towards me cloud your reason — '

'What in heaven's name are you talking about, Kay? The circumstances are these. I love you. Yes, I do! But I should have curbed my impulse, my instinct. I shouldn't have taken so much for granted. I dare say it is too much to expect that you could ever feel for me what I've felt for you since almost the first instant I saw you.'

This wasn't happening to her, Kay thought feverishly. This was happening to someone else, or taking place in a dream.

No, it wasn't, her logic told her. This is reality. This is now, bounded by this moment of time, and this room. Simon Nash is holding me in his arms. He has just declared his love for me.

'Simon . . . ' she breathed hoarsely. 'I — I'm tired. I'd like to go on to bed if you don't mind. This is so — so — '

The trite cliche died on her lips. Simon Nash finished it for her, a trace of bitterness at his mouth.

'Sudden? Surely you really mean that I have astonished you, Kay; taken the ground from under your feet as it were?'

She laughed shakily.

'You've certainly done that with a vengeance.'

'And you're angry?'

'Good lord, no! Angry? No, I'm not in the least angry. You described my present condition pretty well. Astonished.'

'You never expected that I could fall in love with you? Perhaps you imagined I was incapable of ever falling in love again.'

'Caroline.' Kay whispered. 'You loved her.'

'Yes, I did. I thought too it would be

impossible for me to love another woman.'

'But you can't be sure, Simon.' Now Kay felt she should show him a way out of the dilemma. She went on swiftly, 'There is such a thing as infatuation, you know. Oh, I suppose you would call me pretty enough, but — '

'You're not pretty. You're beautiful.'

'All right!' She laughed again without meaning to. 'But there are other pretty women, other beautiful women.'

'Please, Kay! Don't underestimate me, whatever you do. I am aware of all this. Once I was surrounded by beautiful women. You'd say that Nina is a beautiful woman?'

'That glorious redhead? She's certainly beautiful. She made the most of the opportunity to be close to you this evening.'

'We've always been good friends. Once we thought we loved each other. Yes, we did. I believe that Caroline had a similar notion. But this is all digressing from the main point, Kay.

What I happen to feel for you is beyond doubt. What is in doubt is your sentiments concerning me. I may be trying to jump the gun on someone else. Well, you're bound to have a host of admirers.'

'A few,' Kay admitted.

'But you aren't engaged or — or anything like that?'

'No, I'm not, Simon.'

She released herself slowly, brushed a tendril of hair from her forehead in a characteristic gesture. For a moment they regarded each other in silence.

'I'm going to turn in, Simon.'

'Very well, Kay. Goodnight. Thanks for everything. I haven't scared you off Ashleigh?'

She shook her head, hesitated. Doubts began to cloud her mind again, doubts to do with Caroline Nash and the manner of her tragic death. If ever there was an opportunity to attempt to clear the issue, this was it. She let it slide past. The mood was wrong.

'Thank you for dedicating that song to me.'

'It is your song, Kay. Your lyric. Your music.'

'And you'll write others?' she queried tremulously.

'If I do, they will have the same theme running through them. If that isn't possible . . . '

He let the remainder of the sentence go unsaid. Wheeling abruptly, Kay left the room, closing the door firmly behind her. Her legs felt so weak they would scarcely carry her along the passage to her own bedroom. In the sanctuary of her quarters a long shudder ran through her and she collapsed across her bed, her emotions in an absolute maelstrom. It seemed an age went by before she regained equilibrium; even then this was but a pale shade of true balance and perspective.

What a day it had been, to be sure! And with what shattering effect had it been rounded off! A declaration of love from Simon Nash . . . What would Bruce Manson think if he knew? What would Mrs Foley think, Nancy, Simon's sister, and the two children?

'No!' she mused fiercely. 'It's impossible. My place is back home in Westcroft, with my class of children. By right I should pack my cases first thing in the morning and set out on the journey to Westcroft.'

She would do this, she told herself on the one instant, and then on the next she reversed her decision. She couldn't run away and leave everybody in the lurch. What would Diane and Nicholas do if she left them? Any anyhow, what awaited her in Westcroft — an empty house that had ceased to be home on the day her mother died, a handful of friends who could take or leave her? That and the remainder of the holiday months stretching ahead.

'But if I stay,' she whispered. 'What if I stay? What if I remain under this roof, in the proximity of Simon Nash? Where will it all end? Do I love Simon Nash?

Is what I feel for him really love and not simply admiration mixed up with a lot of hero-worship?'

The succeeding hours did nothing to provide Kay with an honest answer. There were too many overtones, too many loose ends that trailed away into doubt and mystery.

Even in the morning she was no nearer to solving the mountainous problem which beset her.

16

For all Kay's indecision, and her reluctance to take the initiative in any way where her relationship with Simon Nash was concerned, events — once set on a determined course by fate — insisted on following that course to whatever conclusion lay ahead.

The succeeding days at Ashleigh took on a new flavour for Kay. The composer, long resigned — or wilfully committed — to remaining a shadow in the background of all that took place at his home in which he was not immediately involved, suddenly emerged as a different personality, with different values and attitudes and an entirely fresh outlook. It was as though he had thrown off the last vestige of the cloud which had surrounded him since the death of his wife.

More often than not, he would leave

the house in the mornings with Kay and the children, joining them in the long rambles and explorations, and evincing a boyish enthusiasm that was sharply at variance with his former apathy. If Kay and Diane welcomed the transformation and its results, it was Nicholas who produced the most touching reaction.

'This is how you used to take me for walks before, Dad. Remember? I was a lot smaller then and had to walk faster than you to keep up with you. Then I'd get tired and you'd have to carry me on your back.'

'Naturally I remember, young man. And I used to carry you so.'

With this he had hoisted the boy to his shoulders and Nicholas gave vent to a gay cry, his eyes shining with pleasure.

At the outset Kay felt vaguely uneasy and found it necessary to make a real effort to adapt to the new conditions. She had the feeling that Simon was endeavouring in his own fashion to wipe out the confusion and embarrassment she had suffered that night in his studio, in order to show her that he could forget the incident if she was willing to do the same.

They might have been brother and sister on those early outings with the children, and while the cultivation of this illusion helped Kay towards a more relaxed manner in his company, yet she felt that by a recognition of their artificial roles they were deliberately sacrificing the blossoming of a deeper and more valuable friendship.

It was as if the composer were saying in effect, 'All right, if I'm not acceptable in one form, then I shall conceal my real self and meet you on whatever footing you care to dictate.'

As one day followed another however, Kay was forced to relinquish her impressions and to acknowledge that Simon was not really playing the role at all, but was being himself — the person he used to be prior to the tragedy that had befallen him.

Finally she gave herself up whole-heartedly to enjoying his company, laughing with him when he laughed, being serious when he was. Gradually they formed a deep respect for each other and a mutual understanding which — whether or not she chose to ignore it — was the commencement of real love for Kay.

In the meanwhile he carried on with his composing, usually in the evenings when the children had gone to bed and the house had settled down for the night. Despite his invitations for Kay to drop into his studio when she had a mind to, she never went near it again. The memory of that night was still startlingly clear and disturbing, and she imagined that, were there to be a repetition of the declaration of his sentiments towards her, she would not be strong enough to resist, much less reject them.

Hal Lambert was a frequent visitor at Ashleigh during this period, as were Bruce Manson and Simon's sister,

Lorna. Oddly enough, Lorna failed to share in the resurgent spirit of hope and enthusiasm which pervaded, and Kay wondered why. She grew bold enough one evening to put the question to the girl.

'Am I not happy with what is happening to my brother?' the slim, fair girl echoed, for a moment thrown off balance by the bluntness of Kay's query. At the same time her eyes ran over Kay in a queer way. There was a glow in them that had escaped Kay on the other occasions she had talked to her. 'Well, now when I come to think of it, I'm not sure that I am,' she confessed.

Kay stifled a gasp of surprise. Curiosity drove her to press Lorna for an explanation.

'I fail to understand you, Lorna. When Simon was idle and depressed you wished he would pull himself together. Now he has pulled himself together, and surely you must be happy for him.'

Lorna was silent for a space while she submitted Kay to another appraisal. Then suddenly it came to Kay what the girl might be thinking of her and her brother. Her cheeks flamed at the idea. Before she could say anything, Lorna beat her to it, talking in a monotone that seemed an odd contrast with her customary mode of speech.

'Are you in love with Simon, Kay?'

Had the girl thrown a bombshell, the effect on Kay could not have been more shattering. While she dithered in confusion Lorna continued.

'Then you are in love with him, my dear Kay — '

'But I didn't say that,' Kay blurted.

'There is no need to say it,' the girl returned, producing a cigarette case from her purse and withdrawing two cigarettes. One of these she extended to Kay and Kay absently accepted it. 'I can see it in your eyes, darling, in your manner. You have changed yourself, you know.'

'I! Oh, surely not, Lorna! And as for

having fallen in love with Simon — '

Lorna made a brusque gesture that caused Kay's voice to tail away. She stared at Simon's sister.

'Is he in love with you, Kay?'

'What!'

'Please don't sound so alarmed. Please don't attempt to lie to me either, Kay.'

'But I wouldn't lie to you! Why should I lie to you? Oh, good grief, Lorna, you're throwing me into an awful state. Also, you're treating me as if I've been proven guilty of some criminal offence.'

The rising anger in Kay's voice had good effect.

'Forgive me, my dear.' Lorna pleaded. 'I have no right to behave so with you, of course. But it's Simon . . . Well, what I mean is, he had all the trouble and worry that one man can take when he was married to Caroline. He went completely overboard about her. He could see nothing but Caroline! Small wonder then that she managed to wrap him round her little finger. That she managed to keep so many other men in tow without Simon suspecting — '

'But you told him, didn't you?' Kay couldn't help retorting.

The look that Lorna gave her was withering. 'If I did, I was only doing what any sister would have done for her brother. And where did you get this inside information, Kay?' she demanded.

Kay coloured furiously, realizing too late that she had made a mistake in passing on what Bruce Manson had told her. It was as if Lorna could read her thoughts, for on the next instant she added, 'I suppose our cousin, Bruce told you a lot of stuff. He has room to talk — I don't think!'

'It wasn't Bruce.'

'Please don't defend him,' Lorna snapped. 'If Simon were to know how Bruce ran after Caroline . . . '

'This is developing into an absurd brawl,' Kay said thickly in disgust. 'I'd rather not hear any more, if you don't mind. As for what I might think of Simon, or he think of me, it is entirely our own business, you'll have to agree.'

Lorna's eyes sparkled, but she restrained herself with a great effort. 'There, there, dear Kay! We mustn't fight. It is just that I'd hate to be a witness to a recurrence of the misery which Simon has been through.'

Now it was Kay's turn to restrain herself. Here was a side to the girl's character she had never suspected existed.

'Whatever misery may or may not befall Simon,' she replied coldly 'it will not be on account of me.'

Lorna took her leave a short time afterwards. She tried to patch up what was, whether or not she chose to recognize it, a damaging blow to her relationship with Kay. Kay was in no mood to be mollified, and the other girl left in a fine flurry. A few minutes later Simon Nash came into the room.

'Lorna has left?' he said in surprise.

'She didn't even hunt me up to say she was going.'

'She was in something of a temper when she left, Simon,' Kay told him, evading his gaze.

'I see!' the composer said musingly. 'And unless my eyes are deceiving me, you too are in a bit of a steam, Kay. Was it on account of something that Lorna remarked on?'

'I — I'd rather not discuss it, Simon,' Kay replied and turned her head from him. She wasn't quick enough to prevent him seeing how she dashed a tear from her eye. Frowning darkly, he strode across and touched her arm.

'Look at me, Kay,' he commanded.

She swivelled slowly to meet his gaze, mustering a smile that trembled across her features. 'It was nothing, Simon.'

'It must have been something. And knowing the potential packed by my sister, I won't be satisfied until you have told me everything. It had to do with us, Kay?'

'Yes,' Kay admitted in a small voice. 'It had.'

'Well, don't stop there,' the composer urged. 'Is Lorna worried in case we've fallen in love with each other. Is she afraid we'll do something unforgivably silly like getting married, when I'll be wide open for all sorts of humiliation after the gilt has worn off, and you've turned to other men for affection and amusement?'

Kay could only gape at him, her cheeks going suddenly pale.

'I — I — '

'You didn't think I was aware of all this,' the composer continued wryly. 'Well, I am, Kay. I can guess what Lorna said to you. No doubt she blackguarded Bruce and Hal, and practically every other man who had the misfortune to darken the doorway of Ashleigh while Caroline was alive.'

After what seemed an age to Kay she found her voice once more. 'I'd rather not talk about it Simon. Apart from anything else, it is none of my affair.'

If she imagined he could accede to her wish, she was mistaken. Gently he propelled her to a chair, then produced two glasses of sherry, handing her one of them before sinking down on a chair opposite her. His eyes, which of late had reflected nothing but enthusiasm and the joy of living, were grave just then.

'Perhaps it is time we had the whole thing out in the open, Kay,' he began slowly. Kay interpreted his pause as reluctance and hastened to mend the situation.

'There is no need to, Simon.'

'Allow me to differ, Kay. There is a need to explain. At least, I feel compelled to. No doubt you have heard all the stories, and a good deal of the rumours concerning the manner of Caroline's death?'

Kay wanted to deny this in an effort to spare his feelings. Yet she could not bring herself to do so. If Simon wanted to be honest with her, then she could be nothing but honest with him. She forced herself to meet the level gaze he bent on her and nodded.

'It is all in the past, Simon. You don't have to resurrect memories which can only hurt you.'

'The situation is different, Kay,' he replied half-musingly. 'Vastly different. We covered a good deal of this ground before — shortly after you arrived at Ashleigh. We — or at least I — did not go into every detail. I am convinced now that I must. Did you hear also that Caroline's accident might not have been an accident at all?'

A chillness gripped Kay at the question. Was she about to learn what lay at the root of the whole mystery? Did she really want to know what lay at the root of the mystery? More important still, did the composer know the true story of the entire matter?

'Yes,' she answered in a weak voice. 'I did. But — but it was an accident, wasn't it? Oh, I do realize how rumours can spring up and flourish — '

'There might have been truth behind

those rumours, Kay.'

'I see,' the girl breathed tensely. 'Then you believe that someone was responsible for the cabin-cruiser going on fire? You think there actually was someone else on board besides your wife?'

The composer sipped from his glass before replying. He frowned.

'There could have been. The chap who was in the vicinity at the time was sure he saw a second person. The police investigated, naturally, but they never found anyone to fill the bill. There was a theory — which was shared by my sister, incidentally — that this mysterious someone was a strong swimmer, that he deliberately caused the cruiser to catch fire, and, when it looked certain that the boat would sink before help arrived, he swam to shore at some point along the beach. Be all that as it may, I never entertained the notion that Caroline was unfaithful to me. I did know she had men-friends in plenty. Everybody who met her was crazy about her, and that includes Bruce, Hal, and heaven knows how many others. Why shouldn't she have been popular and have lots of admirers? At the time I was popular myself, and I don't mind admitting to having had a horde of women-friends.'

'But — but if someone did kill her deliberately, Simon, they must have had a motive.'

'Yes, and there's the greatest mystery of all. How many times have I asked myself who this person — if he ever existed — was? How many times have I wondered why he wished Caroline to die. There is an answer, of course. Caroline could have had a secret lover who had tired of her and who wanted her out of the way — '

'But you never believed that?'

'Odd as it may seen, no,' was the immediate reply.

'Your wife — Caroline — was she not a strong swimmer?'

'She could handle herself pretty well in the water. But she wasn't an expert swimmer, by any means. Almost everyone else around here is. Even Lorna could have given Caroline lessons, as could Hal or Bruce, or a score of others.'

'Then, Simon, if someone did plan to do away with your wife, that person would have known beforehand her capabilities in the sea? He would have felt reasonably sure that, were she to be left stranded so far from the shore without a boat, she would never be able to make it back to dry land?'

'That is so. Not a very pretty picture to draw, is it?'

'It sounds horrible. Almost too horrible to be true.'

'I wouldn't go that far, Kay. It's a queer old world, if you haven't noticed. Peopled by the oddest characters.'

Kay did not wish to pursue the matter further. It was plain that Simon was every bit as much in the dark regarding the true manner of his wife's death as everyone else.

She finished her drink and rose to leave the room.

'Where are you off to?'

'To bed,' she answered unsteadily.

'You will continue to stay here, Kay?'

'Of course,' she answered at once as their gaze locked. 'I have quite a few weeks to go yet before I can call it quits and go back to Westcroft.'

'How would you react if I said you need no longer feel obliged to remain, Kay?'

Kay swallowed quickly, searching his features for a clue to the real meaning behind his words. She could detect none, and wondered if he intended her to accept what he'd said at its face value.

'What about Diane?' she asked dully.

'You've almost succeeded in convincing me that Diane's preoccupation with the sea has no morbid connotations. For that I am grateful to you also.'

'So the children could get along without me?'

'I dare say they could,' he responded airily. He brought cigarettes from his jacket and lit one casually. The glint in his eye had no manifest meaning for Kay.

'When would it be permissable for me to leave?' she asked in a voice she barely recognized as her own.

'I wouldn't set a time limit. You came of your own choice, and I'd prefer you chose your own time for leaving.'

'You wouldn't mind if I left in the morning? It's practically the end of the week, and — '

'I *would* mind. Terribly.'

Kay repressed a desire to cry out.

'But — but you just said . . . '

'Yes. I know what I just said. I'm giving you a choice, Kay. But do remember that, if you remain here for one more day, you might never have the chance to leave.'

Suddenly Kay realized what he really meant and her breast seemed to constrict until the simple act of breathing was well-nigh impossible.

She ought to go on to the door and flee. Yes, her mind screamed at her, this was the last chance she would have of remaining independent and intact as a person. She and Simon Nash were poised together on the brink of love. If she drew back now she would be safe, and free to go home to Westcroft in the morning. She might regret the step she had taken, might daydream of Simon Nash for a little while afterwards; she might sigh once in a while for the love she could have had but had spurned.

Kay hesitated.

An instant's hesitation was all that Simon Nash required.

He covered the space separating them, held out his arms in a gesture of invitation and pleading.

With a soft cry leaving her throat, Kay flung herself into those arms and they closed on her, encircling her in a hold that told her he would never let her go.

'I love you, Kay . . . '

'Oh, Simon, I love you too. I've fought it. Been besieged by doubts — '

'But for no longer?' he urged gently. 'For no longer, Kay?'

'No, Simon, no! For no longer. I believe in you, trust you. It — it would have broken my heart if I'd had to leave you.'

They laughed for a moment, gazing into each other's eyes. When his lips descended to hers she yielded herself fully and wholeheartedly, knowing that indeed she had at last found true love.

17

George Mallows brought the local weekly newspapers from Lynhaven on Friday morning. As well as the Lynhaven Beacon he brought other weeklies from further afield, and even had a national weekly with him.

'I thought you should see what they're saying, sir,' he said to Simon Nash as he handed over the bundle. 'I took a copy of every paper that had a mention of your name.'

'Thank you, George.' Judging by the gardener's tone, he seemed to think the composer would be considering the bringing of lawsuits for libel against the editors of the papers concerned.

Simon Nash brought the newspapers into the library and lit a cigarette before seating himself on an easy chair and picking up the Lynhaven Beacon first of all. Kay had gone off with the children on their customary ramble, and Nancy and Mrs Foley were both busy with their morning chores.

SIMON NASH INSPIRED BY SCHOOLTEACHER was the Beacon's heading. The sub-heading ran. 'Noted Composer Back In Harness.'

'Good lord! What do these fellows do when they really have to strain their imagination?'

There was a photograph of himself on the front page of the Beacon as well, and below, a photograph of Kay. This shot did Kay less than justice, he felt. The photographer had snapped her without proper warning, with the result that she appeared a trifle startled.

It was the Beacon's local opposition, The Lynhaven Courier, that gave a broad hint of the romance which could be in the air.

COMPOSER NASH AND SCHOOL-TEACHER MAKE MUSIC TOGETHER? was their heading. At least the Courier showed more flair and initiative than the Beacon. All the other newspapers hinted at romance also. A faint smile grooved the composer's mouth as he read item after item. It was odd that not one of the reporters had seen fit to mention the actual new piece of music which was the cause of all the fuss. People were more interested in people than in anything else, and that was that.

The composer's smile turned to a frown when he read a report in the North-East Argus. This harked back to the boating accident and the tragic fate of his wife. The mystery had never been cleared up to the complete satisfaction of the police and the press, the writer stated.

Simon Nash rolled this particular newspaper into a ball and flung it from him angrily. Here it was again, the skeletons being dragged out of the cupboards for their airing. The rumours brought out and dusted and displayed for the eyes and ears of whoever might be interested. And Kay, he thought with a trace of dismay. Was it right to involve her in something that was a mystery and that might forever remain so?

Even as he pondered, the telephone rang and Simon rose to answer it. The caller was none other than his sister, Lorna.

'Have you seen the papers, Simon?' was her opening preamble, delivered in a taut, disapproving tone.

'Yes, I have, Lorna,' the composer answered, the faint smile back at his mouth. 'You don't appear to like what you have read.'

'You and that girl, Simon!' Lorna exclaimed explosively.

'My dear Lorna, what is the matter with you?'

'You know what the matter is, Simon. Oh, how could you! After all, what do you really know of her? I don't deny that she seems a nice enough and decent enough girl — '

'There you are!' her brother laughed. 'You've given her a perfectly reasonable reference.'

'But you aren't in love with her, Simon . . . '

'Why can't I be in love with her?' the composer asked with a perceptible hardening of voice. 'If you want to know, Lorna, I do love her. In fact, I am going to marry Kay. In the very near future, I hope.'

'Have — have you asked her to marry you?' Lorna stammered.

'Not yet. But don't worry. I haven't lost my nerve. I'll get round to it presently.'

'Simon, I wish you wouldn't,' Lorna cried. 'She could very well turn out to be someone like — like — '

'Go on,' Simon urged coldly. 'What are you waiting for? You had a fixation over Caroline, Lorna, and now you're going to behave in the same way over Kay.'

'I tried to warn you before, Simon. You wouldn't listen. You are my brother, you understand. You imagine that you know women, but you don't. Did you know that this girl has been out with Bruce?'

'So what?' Simon replied wearily.

'Look, Lorna, you are a very dear sister, and I'm certain you have my best interests at heart, but don't attempt to run my life for me.'

'I'm sorry, Simon!'

'All right. So am I for taking the big stick to you. But do let Kay and me work out our own destinies. As I said, Lorna, she loves me and I love her.'

'It's your funeral, Simon,' the girl said ominously.

'Oh, do shove a sock in it, old girl. Listen, why don't you hunt up a young man of your own to pester? At least it would keep your thoughts off me.'

'You don't appreciate me, Simon!'

'Of course I appreciate you, Lorna. But let's be fair to everybody. I say, why not drop past this evening and make an effort to get to know Kay better?'

There was a short pause before Lorna replied, saying that she might avail herself of the invitation.

'I'd hate you to get hurt again, Simon,' she ended.

'Goodbye,' the composer grunted

and hung up. To the devil with his sister, he thought then. Why did she persist in interfering in his life? To judge by her behaviour, Lorna might have been his mother instead of his sister. She had not liked Caroline — that had been well enough illustrated by those nasty letters she used to send him when he wasn't at home — and now she was losing no time in informing him of her sentiments concerning Kay.

Simon thrust the cigarette end he had been holding into a nearby ashtray and lit another cigarette. He paused in the act of puffing the tobacco to life, his heart skipping a beat. He froze in the fixed position until the match burned down to his fingers. Even then he scarcely stirred from his thoughts.

'Oh, no!' he groaned finally. 'It isn't possible. It simply couldn't be possible . . . '

Grey-faced, the composer thrust his fresh cigarette into the ashtray also, his eyes reflecting something of the doubt and horror that passed through his mind.

Bruce Manson paid a visit to Ashleigh in the early afternoon. The children were riding their bicycles in the grounds while Kay sat on the rustic seat in the garden where she had them in view for most of the time. As far as Kay knew, Simon was up in his studio. He had told her at lunch time that he wished to do a little polishing on another lyric.

As soon as the children saw Bruce's car they dashed towards it. They talked with him for a few minutes and Kay was witness to a large bag of confectionery being handed over. With this Diane and Nicholas left their bicycles and retired from Kay's view. In another moment a somewhat chastened Bruce was striding towards her.

'Hello, Bruce,' she greeted the young man cheerfully. 'To look at you, one would assume you had met with a minor disaster at least.'

'Not a minor one,' Bruce sighed,

taking a seat beside her. 'A major disaster, my dear girl.'

'Oh! When did this happen?'

'I don't know exactly when it happened,' the other replied. 'But, according to all the newspapers, it is a definite fact.'

Colour began to flood Kay's cheeks.

'Yes, I've seen them myself. Mr Mallows brought a whole armful of papers from town this morning for Simon. George had the notion there was enough material to sue about six different publishers.'

'But no libel has been committed?'

'I'm afraid not, Bruce.'

'You are in love with Mr Music then?'

'Please don't sound so bitter, Bruce,' Kay chided, smiling widely at the young man. 'It's just one of those things.'

'Does he love you, Kay? But there's a silly question for a start. He's bound to love you. Who wouldn't?'

'Oh, come now, Bruce! You don't really love me. We're friends. Good friends. Is there any reason why we can't continue to be good friends?'

'Of course not,' the other grinned, relenting when he noticed how seriously the girl was taking him. 'I came past to offer my hearty congratulations.'

'You did! Oh, Bruce, I could kiss you . . . '

'Let's have it then,' he demanded boldly.

'Why not!' Kay leaned over and kissed him on the cheek. She held her cheek for a return kiss.

'There. We have kissed and made up. Could I offer you a bar of chocolate now?' He brought a box of chocolates to view. 'It should have been flowers, but you have a whole garden of them here.'

'You are sweet, Bruce.'

'Then you are going to marry the lucky blighter?'

'If he'll have me.'

'You mean he hasn't popped the question?'

Kay laughed gaily.

'Not really. Just about, though.'

'And the kids?'

'Do you mean, do they know?'

'Do they?'

'I fancy that Diane suspects a lot. If she does, it's plain that she's taking it well.'

'If you do marry Simon, they'll be a responsibility, Kay.'

'One that I imagine I can cope with,' Kay countered confidently.

'Well, that's something.' Manson paused for a moment while a frown puckered his brow. Kay was quick to notice and asked him what was troubling him. Even as she did so, she had the feeling she already knew what was on his mind.

'Don't you wish to tell me?' she urged.

Before he spoke again, cigarettes were brought out and Kay accepted one. The sun was shining brightly from a blue, serene sky. Birds chirped and bustled in the shrubbery about them, and gulls swooped and cried above the nearby cliffs and the sea. Even so, Kay was aware of an atmosphere of chill and dread, and she wished that Bruce had chosen some other time to call.

'Don't you wonder what happened to Caroline, Kay?' the young man said finally, his voice low and completely grave.

Kay glanced at him sharply before shifting her gaze and catching her breath. At length she nodded.

'Yes, I do. But if it was an accident, Bruce . . .'

'It might not have been,' the other said gently. 'I don't want to spoil your happiness, Kay, but I would like to know if you're prepared to live under such a shadow. Call me a douche of cold water if you will, but the shadow exists.'

Kay forced herself to meet his sober regard. She inclined her head.

'If I have to, I can,' she said. 'And, Bruce, surely you don't wish to plant a doubt in my mind either?'

'Concerning Simon? Good lord, no! I

would never dream of doing anything of the kind. I dare say he came under a certain amount of suspicion as well as the rest of us, but for my money he could never have killed Caroline. It isn't in his make-up to destroy anything.'

'Thank you, Bruce. And it could really have been nothing more than a terrible accident?'

'Of course.'

Manson endeavoured to say this with the greatest conviction, but for all that, Kay could see how he retained a doubt, a doubt she would be extremely foolish not to share.

★   ★   ★

Later there was more fuss at the big house. Hal Lambert arrived with people from the recording company who wished to make a record of Simon's new song at the earliest possible moment. They left in the early evening in a cloud of discontent. The composer explained as they sat down to a meal in the dining-room.

'Hal is too eager to get me on to the market again. He refuses to recognize that I'm still not satisfied with what I've produced.'

Hearing this surprised Kay somewhat.

'Do you envisage making changes?' she asked, at the same time wondering if he could be having second thoughts regarding the entire work.

'Not changes as such. Just a little polish here and there. I was never one to dash off anything and let it go at that. And I do have a reputation to consider,' he added with a smile.

'I understand. And it's natural that Hal should be slightly impatient. Possibly he finds it hard to believe that you're actually back in business. He fears he might not get his hands on the song after all.'

'He'll get it,' Simon assured her. 'But he must be patient. If he can wait for nearly three years for results, then another few days won't hurt him.'

The meal over, Kay had declared her

intention of diverting the children for an hour when the composer thought of something.

'Some representatives of the recording company are throwing a little party for me tonight, Kay. I'm sorry to tell you it's strictly a stag affair, which indicates to me they've just dreamed up a new way of cornering me to talk business.'

'You must go in any case,' Kay smiled. 'And even if female friends were invited, someone has to stay at home with the children.'

'You don't mind?'

'Of course I don't. You should have withdrawn from your shell long ago, Simon.'

'I think I'm re-learning fast,' he grinned. 'Do you know, Kay, I could kiss you.'

'Not now, please!' she laughed.

'Oh, yes. I knew there was something else. Lorna might visit tonight. If she does, it will give you someone to chat with. But take her with a pinch of salt, darling. My sister is possessed with the oddest notions.'

'About me?' Kay asked innocently, and then regretted the query when she saw how Simon frowned briefly.

'Never mind,' he said evasively. 'You can cope with her, I'm certain.'

Simon went off at eight and Kay agreed with Nicholas and Diane that they could watch television with her for a while before turning in at nine.

'Providing that the programme is suitable,' she qualified.

When nine came round she saw the children to their respective bedrooms. She tucked Nicholas up first and then went to say goodnight to Diane.

'Miss Ballard,' the girl said quickly as she was turning to leave. 'Is it true that you and Daddy might be getting married at some time in the future?'

Confusion caught Kay and she thought swiftly in an effort to decide what was the best thing to say. At length she made up her mind that the truth only would serve.

'It is true, my dear,' she confessed nervously. 'We intended to break the news to you very shortly. How — how would you feel about having me around the house on a more or less permanent basis?'

'I'd love it, Miss Ballard. Really I would. You've made Daddy happy again and you'd go on making him happy.'

'I should hope so,' Kay whispered, tears in her eyes. She kissed the girl impulsively before dashing from the room.

She had forgotten all about Lorna Nash until the doorbell ringing sent her into the hall. Mrs Foley called from a bend in the staircase.

'Will you need me, Kay?'

'I don't think so, Mrs Foley. It's probably Simon's sister. He said she might call.'

The woman bade her goodnight and Kay continued to open the front door. It was indeed Lorna Nash who stood on the step. The look she gave Kay had a certain restraint about it, Kay imagined. She greeted the girl and asked her in.

'Simon has gone out, I'm afraid,' she explained as they made for the living-room. 'He's having a meeting or a party, or something of the sort in town with people belonging to the recording company.'

'I see. Then there is no one in the house but you and the cook? The children are in bed?'

'Yes, they are,' Kay replied. 'Could I get you a cup of coffee, or a drink of something stronger?'

'Thank you, my dear I'd love a cup of coffee. But let me fix it myself. Come along to the kitchen and we'll chat there. I believe you and my brother have reached a — an arrangement of sorts?'

Kay coloured at the terminology; nevertheless she managed to retain her composure.

'I'm afraid everyone is making the most of what the newspapers had to say, Lorna — '

'Oh, I didn't depend on the newspapers for my information, Kay darling. I had it straight from the horse's mouth, so to speak. At least I had it from one of the horses,' she added with a cruel laugh.

The next ten minutes were a strain for Kay, yet she was determined not to allow Lorna's obvious resentment of the news to hurt her.

'Congratulations anyhow, Kay, my dear. I'm sure you'll both be very happy.'

'Thank you, Lorna.'

'Now I must see if the children are asleep. If Diane is awake she would never forgive me if I didn't say hello to her.'

Kay didn't think this necessary or desirable, but she refrained from making a comment that might have Lorna really baring her nails.

'I shan't be a moment,' she said to Kay and slipped away from the kitchen.

She returned much faster than Kay imagined she would, pale of face and plainly concerned.

'Kay, the child isn't in her bed! Something must be playing on her mind. The front door is open too. Would she try — '

'The cliffs!' Kay cried in terror. 'She has gone to the cliffs. We must get to her before something happens.'

'I'll go with you.' Lorna said and dashed on Kay's heels towards the front door that was indeed lying open.

18

Once the idea had taken root in her mind, Kay never paused to consider the possibility that she might be wrong, and that Diane had not gone near the cliffs or the beach. The open front door seemed to bear out all her fears, and now she raced towards the cliffs with Simon's sister hurrying in her wake.

The evening had dulled, and night had come with leaden skies that made the scene much darker than it would normally have been at this time of year. All the same, when Kay gained the top of the flight of stone steps leading down to the beach, she found she could see the beach itself quite clearly. There was no sign of Diane. Just then Lorna halted beside her, breathing easily enough in spite of the effort she had put in. They peered around them before their gazes met. A nervous laugh escaped Kay.

'She isn't here. I must have been mistaken. But you've heard how she often goes to the beach alone?'

'Yes,' Lorna said. 'I know. Simon always feared she would drown as her mother did.'

Something in the girl's voice sent an icy chill running through Kay. She moved from the top of the flight of steps. Lorna had scrambled through the out-jutting rocks that comprised the peaks of the cliffs. Down there was a hundred-feet drop, at the bottom of which the sea boiled and leaped in a wild frenzy.

'Come away from there, Lorna! If you should happen to fall, you'd break your neck.'

'I think I see something, Kay,' the other girl cried excitedly. 'Yes, I'm sure I do! But I'd lose my balance if I ventured any further. I haven't a very good head for heights.'

'You come back and let me see,' Kay

urged. 'Oh, it could be Diane . . . She might have come along here and slipped.'

Lorna scrambled back from the narrow shelf and Kay edged past her to gain a better view of whatever it was she thought she had seen. Down below her was nothing but a spill of jagged rocks, with the sea frothing angrily beyond.

'What did you see, Lorna?'

'You'll have to go out a little further.'

'But you didn't go so far. And what if I should lose my footing and fall?'

'You'd be killed, my dear, wouldn't you?'

With a gasp of horror choking in her throat, Kay wheeled on her delicate perch to look at Simon's sister. What she saw in the girl's eyes convinced her that this was a trick, that Lorna had deliberately manoeuvred the situation to suit her own ends. Another thought flashed through her mind at that instant. Caroline! Had it been Lorna who had been with Simon's wife that day on the cabin cruiser? Lorna who had hated Caroline so much that she felt she had to murder the woman somehow? And now she was going to kill her, for no other reason than that she and Simon were in love with each other. It meant that Lorna was sick, or that she was possessed with some evil. Perhaps these meant the same thing. There was no time to work it out, Kay told herself despairingly.

'Diane isn't here at all?' Kay panted, fighting desperately for time. Bruce Manson might come along. Mrs Foley might suspect that something was the matter and come along. Or Simon himself may come home from town early . . .

Lorna edged closer to her. The girl had her back to the protection of a squat boulder, so that she was safe enough. Not so Kay. On no side was there a foothold or a handhold. There was no way to go but forward into the grey void and the jagged rocks beneath her.

'Diane is safely in bed, my dear.'

'You — you want me out of the way, Lorna. But why, why!'

'You're no better than she was. She played him false and she paid for it. You are not going to have the opportunity of making his life a misery.'

'But you're wrong,' Kay cried. 'Wrong!'

At that instant her nerve broke and she yelled loudly for help. As she did so she dashed back at Lorna, hoping that by some chance she might wrestle the girl aside.

Lorna was strong and wiry, and it seemed that a demon was rampant in her. She countered Kay's attack and heaved. Then Kay was released and was free, and was falling towards certain disaster.

★ ★ ★

Mercifully, her fall was broken by a rock snag. The most she had suffered, she believed, was bruised ribs. The perch where she crouched was some ten feet below the shelf which had been her original vantage point. On falling she had lost consciousness — fainted. Now she was in possession of her faculties, and was able to feel the chill nip that had entered the air, see the daylight fading and the shadows of night encroach, sense the danger that still threatened should this out-thrust of rock give way, or should she make a false move that would precipitate a downward plunge to her doom.

For how long had she lain here? Where was Lorna? When would someone come to rescue her?

It was full dark, and Kay's courage had reached its lowest ebb, when she heard footsteps on the cliff edge above her. She tried to call out, but whatever feeble sound she made was caught up in the roar and tumble of the waves beneath her, and in the din of the freshening breeze.

Suddenly she heard an anxious cry.

'Kay! Where are you?'

'Simon!' she screamed with all the

power of her lungs. 'I'm here! Down here . . . '

She must have fainted again. There was a period of darkness when nothing at all registered. Then she was being gathered up in someone's arms. She had the vague sensation of being carried, and when she opened her eyes to full awareness once more, she was in the living-room of the big house, lying on a couch while a drink was eased between her lips.

'Are you all right, Miss Ballard?'

The anxious voice was Diane's. She stood in her dressing robe a little to the left of her father. Kay focused on the girl's face and nodded, mustering a smile from she knew not where.

'What happened to you, Miss Ballard?' Diane asked.

'It — it was silly of me. I went for a walk, somehow or other managed to slip and tumble into the rocks.'

'You might have been killed, Miss Ballard.'

'Well, she wasn't,' Simon said gruffly.

'Now, back to bed with you, sweet-heart.'

'Goodnight, Miss Ballard.'

'Goodnight, Diane.'

Then she was alone with Simon and he was holding her hands tenderly. An agony of anxiety was reflected in the gaze he bent on her.

'Are you quite sure you're all right, darling? I should get the doctor — '

'No,' Kay objected. 'Please don't.' She heaved herself upright to prove she had not been harmed. 'Simon . . . where is Lorna?'

'With Mrs Foley,' he returned grimly. 'She was hysterical when she came in. She admitted everything. She must be out of her mind. At the very least she is suffering from some neurotic disorder — has been for years.'

'What are you going to do, Simon?'

'I don't know. I'm taking Lorna to hospital for sure. She — she caused Caroline's death that day, Kay. She told me all about that as well. She planned it carefully, watched at some cove along the beach. She couldn't tell me all the details, but she'll have to tell all to the police . . . '

'Please don't be too hard on her, Simon. I don't intend to think badly of her. If she was sick, then she can't be held responsible. As far as I'm concerned, I did take a walk along the cliffs and slipped.'

'But you can't do that, Kay. She deserves to be punished.'

'No, Simon. Don't you see . . . now you know everything. There is no longer any mystery. The nightmare you have been living in is gone forever.'

'Kay,' he said hoarsely, 'tell me one thing. Do you still love me? Will you still marry me?'

'If you'll have me, darling.'

They clung tightly for a long moment, Simon clutching her as though he would never let her go. They were together and they would always be together.

'Now, Simon,' she whispered presently, 'you'd better see how Lorna is.

Then we must get her to a doctor and hospital. And you don't really condemn her, do you?'

'If you say not to, then I won't.'

'You mustn't, Simon. You mustn't. Whatever has happened in the past, a little good has come out of it.'

'I understand, Kay.'

He held her gently, touching her lips with his own. For Kay too the nightmare was over. Tomorrow would be a new day. Their future lay ahead of them, full of promise, bright as the most golden of dreams . . .

THE END

Other titles in the
Linford Romance Library:

FORSAKING ALL OTHERS

Jane Carrick

Dr Shirley Baxter, after several inexcusable mistakes, leaves her London hospital to look after her sick grandfather in Inverdorran. However, with the help of locum Dr Andrews, he soon recovers. Shirley meets and falls in love with Neil Fraser who is working hard to build a local leisure centre. But Neil's plans are beset with problems, and after he suffers a breakdown, Shirley finds her medical training is once again in demand.

FORBIDDEN LOVE

Zelma Falkiner

By the time Lyndal Frazer learns the identity of the stranger who rescued her and her sheepdog, Rowdy, from drowning, it is too late. She has fallen half in love with a sworn enemy of her ailing father. Torn between growing attraction and duty, Lyndal chooses family loyalty. But Hugh Trevellyn has made up his mind, too; a bitter feud will not be allowed to come between them.

A MAN TO TRUST

Angela Dracup

Alexa Lockton has a thriving car business and her fiancé, Royston Wentworth, is an eminently suitable future husband. But when she employs Rick Markland to work in her garage, her ordered world crumbles. Against Royston's cautious prudence, Rick encourages bold expansion at Lockton's. Alexa is caught between the two men — for she finds that Rick is compellingly attractive and, as she plans her forthcoming marriage, she begins to wonder how long she can resist his magnetic appeal.